TALMAN'S WAR

Jim Talman figured he had trouble enough with drought drying up his water and threatening his herds. That was until Philip Olsen, a man greedy for land, cast his eyes on the Talman range. Jim soon found that talk wouldn't solve the problem — and realised that the only way to hold onto his land was to fight for it.

Books by Richard Wyler
in the Linford Western Library:

BRIGHAM'S WAY
JACOB'S ROAD
TRAVIS

RICHARD WYLER

TALMAN'S WAR

Complete and Unabridged

LINFORD
Leicester

First published in Great Britain in 1976

First Linford Edition
published 2007

British Library CIP Data

Wyler, Richard
    Talman's war.—Large print ed.—
    Linford western library
    1. Western stories
    2. Large type books
    I. Title
    823.9'14 [F]

    ISBN 978–1–84617–930–3

Published by
F. A. Thorpe (Publishing)
Anstey, Leicestershire

Set by Words & Graphics Ltd.
Anstey, Leicestershire
Printed and bound in Great Britain by
T. J. International Ltd., Padstow, Cornwall

This book is printed on acid-free paper

Especially for my wife — Marlene — who makes it all worthwhile.

1

Jim Talman glanced up from his breakfast as he heard his wife calling him. Pushing himself away from the table he went outside. Though it was early the sun was high, the heat already close to uncomfortable. It caught Jim as he stepped through the kitchen door and crossed the dusty yard.

'Trouble?' he asked. His wife was standing beside the low stone wall that rimmed their deep well.

Ruth Talman brushed a few stray damp hairs away from her face then pointed down the dark shaft. 'It's nearly dry, Jim.'

As he stared down the well Jim felt a rise of bitterness. As if they hadn't already had enough bad luck for one year. A drought was the last thing anyone in the basin had expected. This was the middle of the third dry month,

1

and the weather showed no sign of change. Day after day was the same; the sky hard and blue, cloudless, with the air heavy from the constant, pressing heat. Water was becoming more than scarce; the land lay dry, its surface split and cracked. The lack of moisture had turned the grass brown and lifeless. For any community a drought was serious. In cattle country it was liable to become disastrous.

Jim Talman was still among the lucky ones up to now. The western borderline of his range took in a line of high-rising hills. There was still grass up there, though even that was threatening to become scarce. High up in the hills a stream broke out of some underground source, tumbling down the wooded slopes to form a wide creek by the time it reached the flatlands. Jim Talman had counted on this to keep him out of trouble, to keep his herd supplied with the water they needed. He hadn't reckoned with the duration of the drought, and now he was beginning to realise that his own share of worry was about to come due.

He took in the fact now and shouldered it easily. He had been born in this country, born into the cattleman's world, and he bore the ever-present problems with the casual deliberateness that was tradition with his kind. It didn't mean he wasn't aware of the trouble he was in — just the opposite: he knew but he didn't let it grind him down.

'If this does dry up we'll have to start hauling our water up from the creek,' he said to Ruth.

'And when the creek dries up?' she asked.

Jim gave a quick grin. 'Don't let's jump until the whip cracks,' he told her. 'Now you go back inside and don't worry. You'll have your water.'

Ruth kissed him on the cheek and made her way back to the house.

In the time it took his wife to reach the house Jim had decided what he wanted to do. Crossing the yard he opened the door of the cook-shack, the mingled odours of fried bacon and strong coffee reaching him as he stepped inside.

'Mornin', boss,' called Dicken Hodges, the cook, from his kitchen. 'You want some coffee?'

'Why not.' Jim paused in the kitchen doorway as Hodges filled a tin cup. 'How you doing for water?'

Hodges peered at him through a haze of steam. 'Was going to see you about that, Jim. Well's gettin' low.'

'I know,' Jim told him. 'Missus just had me out to have a look.'

'Well, I reckon I've got enough on hand to see me through today.' A hard-done-to tone crept into the old man's voice. 'I do my best but I can't promise what can't be done.'

'Don't fret on it,' Jim said. 'We'll keep you happy.'

Hodges bobbed his head. 'Well I hope so.'

Jim took his coffee over to the long table where his ten-man crew sat eating breakfast. Helping himself to sugar he spent a few minutes swapping words with his hands.

'Andy,' he said to his foreman, 'I want a couple of the boys to stay behind this morning.'

Andy Jacobs, a medium-height, stocky-built, forty-year-old nodded. 'You want anyone in particular?'

'No. I just want two men to root out some big barrels, scald them out, and then take them down to the creek.'

'We needing water, Jim?'

'Yes. The well's starting to dry up.'

'That bad?'

'Could be.' Jim drained his cup. 'So we'd better be prepared.'

The men were finishing breakfast now, moving away from the table. Jim went outside with Jacobs. As they walked across the yard Jim said, 'I think it's time to start moving the herd up into the hill pasture, Andy.'

'I figured that was coming,' Jacobs said. He was lighting his first thin, black cigar of the day. 'I'll get the boys on it right away.'

'A couple of days see it done?'

Jacobs nodded. 'Herd's pretty well bunched. This kind of weather they stick close together, as close to the water as they can. We should be able to have them moving into the hills by tonight.'

They were beside the big corral now, with the crew busy roping and saddling their horses for the work ahead. Dust was boiling up in misty clouds, partly obscuring men and animals.

'I'm riding into town this morning,' Jim told his foreman.

'Looking for hired help?'

Jim nodded. 'We need a couple of good hands.'

'I'll agree on that,' Jacobs said. He ground out his cigar beneath the heel of his boot. 'We need some rain a damn sight more though.'

Jim raised his eyes to the sky. He saw exactly what he'd been seeing for weeks. It seemed an eternity since there had been a cloud to break the sweeping expanse of hard blue. No cloud. No dark banks bringing the hope of rain. Not even a breath of wind.

'This is a godawful country at times, Jim.' Jacobs spoke almost bitterly. 'Times are when a man can knock his head against a wall to figure it out.'

'Dad used to say the only way is to ride with it,' Jim said.

'Your pa generally knew what he was talking about.' Jacobs spoke now with the respect of a man who had been more than just an employee. He had worked for Jim's father, John Talman, for nearly twenty years, hiring on when the Rocking-T brand was laid on the first small herd. He had worked and sweated through the early lean years, and the bad times had been hard until Rocking-T became stable, able to pay its way. Jacobs had gone without pay many times during the early days, and there had been times when even food had almost ceased to exist for the people of Rocking-T. Somehow, though, they lived through it all, and

Andy Jacobs had been part of Rocking-T all the way — helping to build, becoming inseparable from it in the process. He was one of the old breed; loyal to the brand he had worked for to a nearly fanatical degree; when Rocking-T was hurt he felt it; when the brand bled he bled with it.

'This time it's my turn to make the right moves,' Jim said.

Jacobs glanced at him. 'You're John Talman's son,' he said. 'That's all I need to know.' He settled his stained hat square, then turned to where the crew were leading their saddled horses out of the corral.

Back in the house Jim found Ruth clearing away the breakfast things. She gave him a warm smile as he came in.

'I've set a couple of the boys to hauling water up from the creek,' he told her.

Ruth didn't speak for a minute. When she did her face was serious. 'Jim, how long can we last without rain?'

He crossed over to her, taking her in his arms. Ruth pressed herself close, suddenly glad of his nearness.

'I'll be honest, Ruth, and that means I don't surely know. We're moving the herd up into the hills today. That'll give us some leeway. After that — well, I guess it's going to be a case of hanging on. If the creek holds out I think we'll survive.'

'And if it doesn't?'

Jim had no answer to that and Ruth didn't press it. She knew her man, knew the responsibilities he carried. He was a big man, young and strong, but too much at one time could break even the strongest. And Ruth Talman was too much of a woman to be the cause of it to her own husband.

'Are you still going into town?' she asked, changing the subject.

'Yes. Why? You want something?'

Ruth smiled. 'I have a small order you can pick up for me from the store.'

'That means I'd better hitch up the wagon,' Jim said, his face dead-pan.

He could still hear Ruth's laughter in his ears when he turned his horse away from the corral an hour later and put it on the trail that led across Rocking-T range to the small town that served the outlying cattle community.

Away from the buildings the sun was stronger; it cut through his shirt and a patch of sweat formed down his back in minutes, soaking through the faded denim. Jim rode slowly, letting his horse set its own pace. He had an hour of riding ahead and there was no use in pushing his horse without need. He rolled a smoke, hoping to blot out the taste of dust that tainted his every breath.

Rocking-T range spread out around him in every direction. It was good land, Jim thought. He stared at the hostile sky for a time. If only they could get some rain. What should have been lush grazeland was now shrivelled and dried-out, the grass brown, the earth hard and dusty. Trees and brush stood motionless in the hot air. There wasn't even a breeze to stir the leaves.

He spotted a couple of his hands hazing a big bunch of steers up out of a brush-filled hollow and rode over to talk to them. He ran a knowing eye over the beeves as they jostled slowly by. The drought was beginning to leave its mark on them. The steers were looking thin, and Jim was able to count a rib or two. The hill pasture was his last hope. His herd needed fattening up before too long passed. The cattle markets wanted prime beef, not skin and bone on the hoof.

Riding on for a way Jim dismounted when he reached the creek. The level of the water was down some he noticed. He looked upstream, following the meandering path the creek had cut. Some way up he saw the ranch wagon pulled in under some trees while two of the hands manhandled buckets of water into the big barrels tied down on the wagonbed. Jim took a quick drink then mounted up after his horse had taken its fill. He let the animal ease through

11

the water and up the sloping bank on the other side.

On this stretch of Rocking-T there was a lot of timber. Jim rode through deep growths of tall trees and tangled brush. It was a shade cooler in amongst the high trunks and interwoven branches which formed a green canopy to hold back a lot of the heat. Here it was dim and shadow-dappled, with pale beams of sunlight lancing down through the leaves. It gave an atmosphere of misty coolness to the place, and Jim was grateful for the temporary relief from the open heat. His horse made no sound on the carpet of thick, fallen leaves as it passed, and from high over his head a bird broke into song. The sound reached down to Jim and he raised his eyes towards the source. It was a pleasant sound coming down from the high emptiness.

He was still listening when a louder, more urgent sound broke through to him. Jim reined in hard, his head coming round in the direction of this new distraction. Reining his horse around, Jim rode into the tall thicket that lay between him and the sound.

As he finally broke out of the trees, coming into the open, a fresh outburst of sound shattered the silence, and Jim brought his sweating horse to a halt, snatching his rifle from the leather sheath on his saddle.

Rage boiled up in him at what he saw before him. A rage so strong he almost lost control. He had his rifle out, cocked and levelled before he realised it. Only then did he clamp down on the flaming anger that was threatening to burst free.

2

Here in this slope-banked, rock-strewn hollow stood a battered canvas-topped wagon, its team motionless in the heat. A small way off two saddle-horses were tethered. In the middle of the hollow a campfire burned, complete with a blackened coffee pot and frying pan. Close by a butchered young steer, wearing the Rocking-T brand, hung suspended from an improvised pole tripod.

Jim saw all these things in a swift, blurred glance as he swung his rifle round onto the tight group of people before him. There were four of them; three men and a woman, more a girl, he realised in the same instant. Two of the men he recognised. Dunc Howser and Cal Jarrett were a couple of lazy and indifferent men who called themselves cowhands. Jim knew to his cost that they were nothing of the kind.

Nearly a year ago he had signed them on at Rocking-T, and he had regretted it ever since, right up to the day when he fired them two months back. Howser and Jarrett had been a thorn in his side from the day they'd come to work for him. Work-shy and slovenly, they had wasted time and money for Jim Talman, and it had dragged on until Jim had had enough. His crew had been fed up with the way the pair carried on, and Jim knew it wasn't fair to expect his regular, hard-working crew to tolerate it. Besides that it was getting to be a day-long chore, keeping track of them. When Howser and Jarrett weren't slacking on the job they were in town drinking and getting into fights. Rocking-T began to get a bad name, and that was when Andy Jacobs had come to Jim about the pair. It hadn't taken long to reach a decision. Jim had made up what wages were due and had gone over to the bunkhouse. There had been a lot of swearing and threats from the two, but there was nothing they could do with the entire Rocking-T crew looking on. Gathering up their gear Howser and Jarrett had ridden out. Jim had seen them in town from time to time. Once or twice trouble had almost reared its head, but up until now nothing had come of it.

Now Howser and Jarrett were back on Rocking-T range. Why they were here was self-evident; the camp, the tethered horses, the slaughtered steer. It was an obvious strikeback at Rocking-T.

Who the others were was a mystery to Jim Talman at the moment. But it was clear that they were not friends of Howser and Jarrett.

The third man, in his early fifties, judging by his looks, was on his knees, pinned there, helpless in the grip of the powerfully bulky Cal Jarrett who had a thick arm around the man's throat. Blood was dribbling freely down the man's face from a gash on his left cheek. Yet despite his obvious helplessness the man was struggling against Jarrett's hold on him, and shifting his gaze Jim could see why.

Dunc Howser was a heavy slab of a man, and he was as powerful as he looked. The strength he carried made him more than a match for the slim, dark-haired girl he had spread-eagled on the ground. It was more than clear what his intentions were as he reached out a huge hand for the front of the grey dress the girl was wearing. She, to her credit, made no sound now, but put everything she had into fighting against Howser's brutal attack.

It only took Jim a few seconds to see and realise the situation, and as yet he hadn't been spotted. Knowing this Jim kicked his horse into movement towards the four. He had no precise plan of action. It was just a case of pitching in and figuring it out later.

As the bulk of Jim's horse loomed close by, Cal Jarrett became aware of its presence. His head snapped round, eyes wide as he saw the shape of man and horse lunging towards him. He tried to yell a warning, letting go of his captive and grabbing for his handgun. He was too slow. Jim Talman's heavy boot, free of the stirrup, drove at him. It caught him in the chest. Jarrett's cry was cut off in his throat as he went over onto his back, the breath smashed from his body.

Jim saw Jarrett fall away as his horse carried him on. He felt no emotion but anger, no thought of what he might do, or what the outcome might be, as he used his rifle like a club on Dunc Howser. If anything he felt a rush of satisfaction as the sun-glinting barrel chopped down across Howser's hatless skull. A howl of pain burst from Howser's lips and he forgot all about the girl as he raised his head to search out his attacker. When he saw who it was he shoved to his feet, his lips peeling back from his teeth in a snarl of pure hate for Jim Talman.

Jim hadn't expected any resistance from Howser; he realised that he hadn't allowed for Howser's enormous reserves of strength. Reining his horse about Jim knew he had to finish this now. Howser wouldn't let it go. Jim threw a quick glance towards Cal Jarrett; Howser's partner was still where he had fallen, obviously out of the game for the time being. Bringing his attention back to Howser, he found the man already on his feet. No more than a couple of yards separated the two, and though he still held his rifle, Jim knew he couldn't use it. He knew also, that Howser would not think the same way. And Dunc Howser confirmed this the next instant as he reached for his handgun.

With bare seconds left to him Jim made his move. He let go of his rifle, kicked his boots clear of the stirrups, and gigged his horse forward. Closing in on Howser, Jim launched himself out of the saddle. His right shoulder took Howser high in the chest, and the two men went down hard. Jim rolled clear, pushing to his feet. Dust stung his eyes.

He eased forward, not wanting to let Howser get his balance. He grabbed Howser's shirt front and yanked the man upright. He only remembered Howser's gun when the weapon swept up in a deadly arc. Jim jerked his head aside as Howser brought it down — the barrel of the gun missed his skull but caught him on the side of the neck. The blow was hard, briefly numbing. Howser lifted the gun again, trying for a second strike. This time Jim was ready. He let Howser raise the gun, then he drove a sledging right into Howser's ribs, following up with his other fist, which caught Howser full in the mouth. With his lips split and bleeding, Howser backpedalled. He seemed to have forgotten the gun in his hand. Spitting blood he pawed at his numbed lips, staring vacantly at the red wetness that streaked his fingers. And he was still staring at it when Jim stepped in and drove a swinging right at his head — the blow was delivered with the whole of Jim's strength and it struck with a loud, meaty sound. Howser spun on one heel and then fell onto his face.

Jim scooped up Howser's handgun, then moved over to collect Jarrett's weapon. Howser's partner was still where he had fallen, his unshaven face a sickly white. His breathing was harsh and rasping. Jim placed the confiscated weapons in his saddlebags and retrieved his own rifle.

Only then did he turn his attention to the girl and the older man.

3

The man's name was John Dobbs and the girl was his daughter Melanie. They were on their way to town to move into the recently vacated general-store, the previous owner having sold out to Dobbs and then heading out for the California gold-fields. On their way to take over the store, the Dobbs had got lost during the previous night and had come upon Howser and Jarrett. They had only stopped to ask the way. Giving directions wasn't enough for Howser or Jarrett, and Jim Talman had arrived just as things were turning unpleasant.

Dobbs wasn't badly hurt. His wound looked worse than it felt. After assuring him she was all right, his daughter went to their wagon. She returned with cloth and a bowl of water and set to cleaning up the gash on her father's cheek.

While this was going on Jim wandered over to the butchered steer. Obviously Howser and Jarrett had been aiming to set themselves up with a supply of meat. Anger rose again as Jim stared at the carcase. Damn them, he thought, was he going to be plagued by this pair now? He was going to have to lay the law for them here here and now, he realised.

Jarrett was slowly recovering. He sat up, rubbing his chest, and as Jim moved over to stand before him he looked up. His face, though still pale, was cold and hard.

'You like to caved in my chest,' he said. His voice was ragged, husky.

'Next time it'll be your neck,' Jim told him. 'I could hang you now and I don't think anyone would raise an objection.'

'Hang!' Jarrett's voice was suddenly shrill with indignation. 'What for?'

'For stealing and butchering one of my prime beeves. For assaulting that girl over there. You know damn well the way folk feel about rape around here.'

Jarrett gave a pasty leer. 'Hell, it weren't rape. Was only a little fun.'

Jim put the muzzle of his rifle to Jarrett's forehead. 'Say that again, Jarrett. Say it so I can blow your head off.'

For a few seconds Jarrett stopped breathing. Terror showed in his eyes and an oily sheen of sweat broke out over his face. He stared at Jim and he knew he'd said the wrong thing.

And then Jim jerked his rifle away. 'Get out of here,' he said, his voice edged with bitterness. 'And take that scum you call Howser with you.'

Jarrett scuttled away from Jim. Crossing to the tethered horses he began to saddle them up. When he'd done he moved over to the fire to collect up the tinware, but Jim waved him off with his rifle. Scowling, Jarrett began to protest, then thought better of it. He turned to the unconscious Howser. He jammed Howser's hat back on, then dragged his partner to the waiting horses. After a lot of pushing and swearing he got Howser slung across his saddle.

'What about our guns?' Jarrett asked. He was on his own horse now, his face sullen, half-defiant.

'I'll leave them in Sheriff Nolan's office. Collect them from there. But stay out of my way.' Jim moved in close to Jarrett's horse. 'One thing. Tell this to Howser when he wakes up. If I see either of you on Rocking-T after today you'll be shot. On sight. I'm issuing that order to my crew, and it's for real.'

'You can't do that,' Jarrett burst out. 'You can't shoot a man just for riding on your ra . . .'

'Can't I?' Jim cut in on him. 'Try me then. See whether I mean it or not.' He jerked his rifle. 'Now ride out, mister, and don't look back.'

Jarrett picked up the reins of Howser's horse and led out. Jim stood and watched until men and horses were hidden beyond a low ridge. As they disappeared something seemed to snap inside him; tension drained away in a rush and he felt suddenly lightheaded. He knew, though, that it wasn't over yet. Somewhere, someday, there would be a reckoning between himself and those two.

'If you want to lay charges against that pair,' Jim said, turning to face John Dobbs and his daughter, 'I'll back you up.'

Dobbs glanced at Melanie. She coloured and shook her head, eyes downcast. 'I don't think so, Mr. Talman,' Dobbs said. 'Maybe we should, but we'd rather not.'

Jim was looking at the girl. She was trying not to listen. He realised that she wanted to forget the whole thing. He knew that with his evidence to back them up the Dobbs would probably be able to make their charges stick. But if they did it would come out for everyone to hear. Luckily, because of Jim's intervention, it hadn't gone too far, but it would still be revealed in full. Courts had a habit of exposing every detail of a crime in the process of dispensing justice. It was unfortunate, but it was that way. It was plain to see that Melanie Dobbs was the kind of girl who would never be able to live down the aftermath of a court-case. Never mind that she was the innocent victim, people would still talk — they were made that way. Those knowing smiles and pointed stares could bite just as deep as any physical assault.

'We'll forget it then,' Jim said. He crossed over to the still-burning fire. 'Anyone fancy a mug of coffee?'

'Not for me,' Melanie said.

John Dobbs said he would and Jim poured him one, then took one for himself.

'Rest up a while,' he told Dobbs, 'then I'll ride into town with you.'

'Mr Talman,' Melanie said after a while, 'would you have killed those men if it had become the only way out?'

Her father turned to look at her, shock showing clearly on his face. 'For heaven's sake, girl, what a thing to ask.'

'It's all right.' Jim glanced at Melanie over his coffee mug. 'Did I look as if I might?'

She nodded. 'You looked as if you hated them.'

'I've no cause for liking them. They used to work for me. I fired them when I found out they were nothing but shiftless idlers. When I saw them today I guess I just took out all my grievances on them. I suppose I'm pretty well on the edgy side the way things are.'

'The drought you mean?' John Dobbs asked.

'You named it.'

'How bad are things?'

'Bad enough, and apt to get worse if we don't get some rain soon.'

'And if you don't get rain?' Dobbs asked, then gave a mirthless smile. 'I know the answer to that. I've seen cattle-country in droughts before. It's a sad picture, and nobody gains by it. Everybody loses one way or another.' He broke off. 'I guess I'm talking selfishly there.'

Jim drained his coffee. 'We all tend to think of our own positions at a time like this. It's only natural. Why the only thing I'm really bothered about is how long my water supply is going to last.'

It was the truth he spoke, and the problem was still heavy on his mind when he rode into town some time later, with John Dobbs' wagon trailing behind. Kneeing his horse in at the store's hitching rail Jim dismounted, then gave Melanie a hand down off the wagon. She smiled her thanks then made a vain effort to get rid of the dust from her clothing.

'I could get to dislike this country very quickly,' she told him.

'Wait until our rainy season,' Jim said.

She eyed him tolerantly. 'Will it ever come?'

'Maybe,' he told her.

A tall, slim young man had come out of the store, blinking as he emerged from the gloom. He stood on the edge of the boardwalk with one hand raised to shield his eyes from the hard sunlight. He was around twenty-five, but looked older. His pale hair was brushed straight back from his high forehead. His face was thin, his eyes big and wide behind steel-rimmed glasses. He gave the impression of being on the brink of total fright, as if he expected everyone to yell boo at him. His name was Albert Doubleday, and Jim knew that despite his appearance he was a first-rate book-keeper and clerk. He had worked for the previous owner of the store for a number of years, keeping complicated accounts with the ease of a master of his trade. Doubleday also kept the accounts of other places of business in town, and also those of a number of local ranchers, Jim included. In all the time Jim had known him he had never known an instance when Doubleday hadn't been able to come up with complete and accurate lists of all the accounts he kept, and a mistake was something that just didn't exist in Doubleday's world of figures.

'Morning, Albert,' Jim said.

Doubleday glanced at him, peering owlishly through the thick glasses. 'Oh,' he said after a minute, 'why yes, good morning, Mr Talman.'

Jim smiled at Melanie Dobbs. She had a quizzical look on her pretty face. Until people got used to Doubleday's ways he seemed an odd, half-asleep character.

'Albert, this is Mr Dobbs and his daughter, Miss Melanie.'

Doubleday reached out and took John Dobbs' outstretched hand. 'A pleasure, sir.' He turned his attention briefly to Melanie. 'I hope your trip wasn't too uncomfortable, Miss.'

'Thank you, Mr Doubleday,' Melanie answered, giving him a smile that would have made any man look again. But Doubleday had already forgotten her. He was leading her father into the store, avidly talking about trade prospects due to the prolonged drought.

'I don't suppose he's married by any chance?' Melanie asked.

'Albert? No, I'm afraid his only loves are his books and long lines of figures — money type figures, not female.' Jim grinned at her. 'Give him time and maybe he'll get around to noticing you.'

Melanie tossed her dark head. 'Hah. What makes you think I want him to notice me?' She was very definite in her attitude, but there was colour in her cheeks. Nothing made a woman madder than to be totally ignored by a man.

Jim mounted up, gathering the reins. 'I'll be dropping in later,' he told her. 'There're a few things I have to pick up for my wife.'

She nodded, then put out a hand as he prepared to move off. 'Mr Talman — Jim — I just want to say thank you.'

He didn't need to say anything. Touching his hatbrim Jim gigged his horse into motion, heading up the street towards the Sheriff's office.

4

The township of Garnett was one of few that could boast a stone jail. The only other non-wooden structure was the Cattleman's and Mercantile Bank; Jim made a mental note to have a word about money with the bank's president in the near future. If it wasn't a shortage of water it was a shortage of money, or both.

Looping his horse's reins around the hitching rail Jim untied the bulging gunnysack from behind his saddle and stepped up onto the shaded boardwalk before the jail.

Inside the building it was a fraction cooler, but only a fraction. In here the heat was heavy and stifling rather than directly searing. Jim closed the door behind him, cuffing his hat back as he leaned against a rough, whitewashed wall.

Garnett's sheriff, Ben Nolan, eased himself back in his seat and swivelled round to face his visitor. A big, solid man in his early forties, Nolan had been the town's lawman for nearly twelve years. He had been a long-time friend of Jim's father, and had watched Jim Talman grow from a wide-eyed boy into a dependable, married man, an important member of the community. He regarded Jim as more than a friend, in his own mind he saw Jim as the son he'd never had. Nolan's marriage, years back, had been shortlived; his wife had died of smallpox, taking with her the unborn child she was carrying. It had left a gap in Nolan's life that had widened and darkened until he came to Garnett and renewed his friendship with John Talman. For five years he had been deputy to Garnett's sheriff, and on the latter's retirement Nolan had stepped into the top position. Throughout all those years, from the day he'd arrived, Nolan had watched, and with John Talman's approval, had helped to guide Jim's life towards manhood. And when Jim's parents had passed away, within a year of each other, Nolan had found himself taking the place of Jim's father. Jim had been twenty-two then, the last of the Talmans. His father had left him a legacy that needed a big man to command it. Nolan had had no misgivings; he knew Jim well, and his faith had held strong. Jim had taken on Rocking-T without hesitation. Not only that, but he'd made it a success, bringing to fruit all the dreams and plans visualised by his father. Six years had gone by, changing the boy into a proud, capable man of twenty-eight, who now stood in Nolan's office, his brown face somehow troubled.

'You look like a man with a problem,' Nolan said goodnaturedly.

Jim dumped the loaded sack on the floor beside Nolan's battered desk. The lawman glanced down at it, then poked at it with the toe of his boot.

'Well, what is it? You tell me 'cause I

ain't got the energy to bend down and look.'

'Couple of tin mugs, coffee-pot, and a pair of gunbelts and handguns.'

Nolan digested the words for a time. From somewhere out of the paper-strewn disorder of his desk he produced a long, thin cigar which he lit up. When he had the thing going well he returned his attention to Jim.

'And?' he said.

Jim told him, leaving nothing out. His face suddenly hard, Nolan listened in silence. His cigar went out and he relit it.

'I should have run that pair out of town long ago. Only they ain't never done anything that gave me the excuse.' Nolan bit angrily down on his cigar. 'Hell, they just do nothing but cause upset.'

'Ben, you'll let it go, won't you? I promised the Dobbs it wouldn't go any further.'

Nolan eyed him sternly. 'I ain't got much choice, and well you know it, Jim

Talman.' His tone was mixed anger and frustration. 'If the Dobbs won't prefer charges there isn't much I can do. But it's wrong, Jim, damned wrong.'

'Maybe, Ben, but I think I know what the girl feels. It could be hard on her.'

'Yeah, I guess so.' Nolan looked hard at Jim. 'What about your beef?' We could get 'em on that.'

Jim shook his head. 'Right now I got enough problems. Let it go this time, Ben.'

Nolan sighed. 'Ah, what the hell. Jim, you know what your pa'd have done with that pair. He would've hung 'em. Right there and then. No messing.'

'I thought that was the kind of thing you wanted to stop,' Jim answered.

Nolan saw the gleam in his eyes and grinned suddenly. 'Smart boy, ain't you! Hey, how's that lovely wife of yours? I haven't seen her for a while. She pregnant yet?'

'No.' Jim smiled; this was Nolan's standing question. 'We're working on it though.'

'You youngsters are too slow these days.' Nolan pushed out of his seat, crossing to the door. He opened it and placed his big frame in the open space. 'Jim, you figure it's ever going to break?'

'Sometime, Ben, but I don't know when.'

'How you doing at Rocking-T?'

'Feeling the pinch. The boys started moving the herd up into the high pasture this morning. If the creek doesn't dry up I figure we'll be all right.'

Nolan glanced over his shoulder. 'What if it does, Jim?'

Jim couldn't hold back his laughter. 'You're about the fourth person who's asked me that today. Everything seems to revolve around that creek right now.'

'It's the logical question.'

Jim took off his hat and ran a hand through his thick, dark hair. 'Ben, I just don't think that far ahead. If I did I guess I'd worry myself out of my pants.'

Moving outside Nolan stared up and

down the street. Garnett slumbered fitfully in the searing heat. There weren't many people about, only a few horses at the hitching rails. Following on Nolan's heels, Jim handed the lawman his hat. Nolan put it on, squaring its brim.

'I'd better go down and say welcome to Mr Dobbs,' he said.

'You won't change his mind. Or his daughter's,' Jim told him.

Nolan smiled. 'Maybe.'

'Ben, come over to Rocking-T one night for supper. Any night. Ruth'll be glad to see you. It's been too long since you visited.'

'I'll do that, Jim, and thanks.' Nolan touched Jim's shoulder then moved off up the boardwalk.

Jim watched him go, conscious of the feeling he had for the man. Next to his father, Ben Nolan had been the ideal man in Jim Talman's eyes. Now that his father was gone, Jim found he was drawing even closer to Nolan. Despite the fact that he was a man who needed to stand on his own two feet, Jim was glad he had someone like Nolan for a friend; a man had to be able to stand alone — but it sometimes helped if he had a good listener when he wanted to talk; Ben Nolan had moved into the position occupied by the late John Talman. Jim realised this, didn't let it worry him, for he knew where to draw the line, and he knew that Nolan himself would never step beyond that line.

Nolan's distant figure turned into the doorway of the store. Narrowing his eyes against the blinding glare of sunlight on the dusty street Jim led his horse over to the opposite side of the town's thoroughfare. He tied his mount at the hitching rail of the Garnett Palace Saloon. The sign bearing the name was weathered and pale, the wood dried out and beginning to warp. Jim took off his hat and dusted it against his leg. A great many things were going to be dried out before this drought was over, he thought. He realised in the same instant that he was becoming morose, and he couldn't allow that to happen. He stepped up onto the boardwalk and into the saloon. The batwing doors swung noisily on hinges that needed oil. The noise carried outside onto the street, losing itself in the hot emptiness.

Garnett appeared to be slumbering, resting in the bright hotness. It seemed peaceful enough; but there was something in the air, a growing mood of unrest, a brooding swell of menace that had gone unnoticed up to now.

It was not to remain so. A change was due, though it was to have its origins some distance from Garnett itself.

5

Swinging out of the saddle Andy Jacobs
rein-led his horse along the edge of the
creek. His face was grim, his eyes dark
as he paused to study the flow of water.
His suspicions were confirmed to the
full, and Jacobs felt a rise of anger at the
confirmation.

Rocking-T's water was drying up.
But not by any natural happening.
Jacobs had felt his feelings grow
stronger as he had ridden up into the
hills. Now, as he neared the very crest
of the range, he knew what was taking
place. Someone was stealing Rocking-
T's water; someone who had blocked
off the creek's natural flow, diverting it
elsewhere. And Jacobs knew who it was.
He didn't need to be told. He knew as
sure as he knew there was going to be
trouble over this.

Beyond the western edge of Rocking-T

range, on the opposite side of the hills lay the vast, sprawling cattle-empire belonging to Philip Olsen. Rocking-T was big — big by any standards — but Olsen's Boxed-O was gigantic. It spread far and wide, a great tract of land that was too big for its neighbours' comfort. Every ranch in the area was shadowed by Boxed-O's bulk, and the presence of its owner.

Philip Olsen had been beaten to the punch by John Talman in the race for good rangeland. Where Olsen grabbed and held by force, John Talman selected and filed his claim. He secured title on Rocking-T right under Olsen's nose, taking in the range of hills that gave birth to the creek that watered the flatlands below. Olsen had never forgotten this. For a long time Olsen had tried to take over Rocking-T, but John Talman had blocked his every move. Violence had flared once or twice, but it had never gotten out of control through John Talman's handling. It was a clear, but undeclared fact that Olsen wanted Rocking-T. While John Talman lived

Olsen was thwarted every time. His bluster and bellow didn't bother John Talman; now, though, John Talman was gone, and as yet his heir had not had to prove himself — since Jim had taken over Olsen had been unusually quiet. Soon after John Talman's death, Olsen had gone away for three months. When he had returned he'd brought a wife back with him, a young woman of twenty-four, sixteen years his junior. A lot of changes had taken place at Boxed-O since then: new buildings had gone up, the range was restocked with bawling herds of cattle, adding to Olsen's already huge herds. It became obvious that Olsen was intent on building up the largest cattle-ranch in the territory. And it seemed as if he would succeed. He made a couple of financially rewarding drives, selling his beef at record prices. He bought out a couple of smaller brands, adding to his huge range. Yet always, to those at Rocking-T, was the feeling that Olsen's eyes were on them, on Rocking-T's good graze and water. Jim Talman had a spot on his mind that was always alert for any move from Olsen. There were times when he forgot the man altogether — but somehow Olsen was always there, a close-at-hand, lurking threat. Jim knew that one day Olsen would make his play — and when that happened Jim would need everything he had in him to combat it.

Being as much a part of Rocking-T as anyone, Andy Jacobs' thoughts ran along the same lines as his employer's. And as he followed the course of Rocking-T's creek up into the hills he began to realise that Olsen's move was already under way. Jacobs had no qualms at pinpointing Olsen before he had proof. There was no-one else it could be. With the size of herds he ran Olsen was going to face hell in broad daylight during this drought. His need for water would be more than desperate. And Olsen would never tolerate going under, especially if Rocking-T managed to stay alive. It was simply a case of survival — survival of the toughest, the most ruthless. Jacobs saw the beginning of a full-scale range war in the offing. He knew this because just as Olsen would use every trick to get what he wanted, Jim Talman would do just the same to hang on to what was his. Jim was not a strongly violent man, but he would face a threat to his land and life with as much fury as any adversary.

Up ahead, from somewhere in amongst jumbled, eroded rock and tangled brush, Jacobs spotted a thin spiral of smoke rising into the pale sky. Now this fears were justified. Someone was making camp at the source of the creek.

Easing silently into the heavy timber that flanked the banks of the creek Jacobs tied his horse. Sliding his Winchester from the leather sheath, he moved through the dappled shadows of trees and brush, making his way up towards the rocky escarpment where the smoke was still visible.

It took him no more than five minutes, and he found himself almost on top of the smoke before he knew it. From the cover of the undergrowth Jacobs was able to move into the mass of hot, jumbled rock with ease. Here he had to move with extra caution, for any noise would carry loudly amongst the great slabs of tumbled stone.

He heard them before he saw them. First a murmur of voices, then the scrape of a boot against hard rock. A little way off to his left he heard a horse snort. Working his way higher up the sloping rock-face, Jacobs abruptly found himself looking down on a hastily improvised camp. Five men were gathered around a small fire, drinking coffee. Every man was heavily armed. Jacobs saw tools as well — shovels, picks, axes; before they had taken their coffee the five had been busy.

Just beyond where the five sat the ground sloped away to the place from which Rocking-T's creek originated. Bubbling up out of a four-foot fissure into the hardrock the water collected in a broad, natural basin, which in turn flowed over the crest of the hill and down the age-old watercourse to the flatlands below. Now though, the flow-off was blocked by a solid dam of logs and tumbled stone. Some water still got through but it was a mere trickle to what it should have been. On the opposite side of the basin a fresh run-off had been hacked out of the rock, draining the water down Boxed-O's side of the hill.

Jacobs took this in and saw it as nothing less than a death-blow aimed directly at Rocking-T's heart. It was plain to see, and he knew it had to be stopped before it went too far.

He glanced towards the bunched horses. There were five, so it appeared that the five men below were all that were here. If there were others he would just have to be on the alert for them. Whichever way it went, Jacobs decided, his next move was going to start something off that had been brewing for a long, long time.

He thought no more about it. Coming to his feet he brought his rifle to bear on the five men.

'Move easy, gents,' he said evenly. 'Don't give me the excuse I need to shoot.'

They rose as one, seeking his voice. Coffee mugs clattered on hard rock. One spilled its liquid into the fire and it hissed and sputtered a cloud of steam into the air. When they saw the rifle he held, they kept their hands away from their sides — all save one. He was a tall, thin redhead who uttered an oath and went for his holstered Navy Colt. He was fast, but nowhere near fast enough to go against a man holding a cocked gun. Perhaps he had thoughts that Jacobs wouldn't shoot. Plainly he didn't know Andy Jacobs' reputation as a man who never made a statement he didn't mean. It was a mistake the redhead never got a chance to rectify. As his handgun cleared the leather Andy Jacobs triggered off one shot. The redhead's jaw dropped open as the heavy bullet took him just below the hatbrim, above the left eye. His arms flew wide as he spun round on his toes like a dancer. He was already dead when his body struck rock. He rolled until he was almost in the water, lying on his stomach, his face twisted round so that one eye, still open, stared unblinking at the sun.

With the echo of the shot rattling away among the rocks and trees, Andy Jacobs slithered down the sloping rockface, bringing himself onto the same level as the men under his gun. They were still staring at the body of their redheaded companion, and Jacobs took advantage of their shock, placing himself with his back to solid rock before he spoke again.

'All right then, let's have the hardware on the ground.' His tone was hard, snapping out the words at them, and they obeyed meekly. 'Step back, gents, just far enough so I don't have to feel nervous.'

'Damn you, Andy, there weren't no reason to kill Red,' one of the four burst out; Jacobs recognised him, as he had also recognised one other Boxed-O rider. The one who had spoken was a fair-haired, heavy man who went by the name of Curly. To his right stood a young man named Jack Murray. The other two were strangers to Jacobs, as was the man he had shot.

'Why, Curly, you know I had no choice,' Jacobs answered him.

'Olsen ain't goin' to like it. He ain't goin' to look at it that way,' Curly threatened.

Jacobs spat suddenly, his face hardening. 'You can tell Olsen I don't give a damn which way he takes it.'

'This could make a war,' Curly stated flatly. 'And if that happens Rocking-T ain't got a chance.'

'Try it and we'll see,' Jacobs snapped, then realised he was just being drawn into a brag and threat match. He jerked his rifle in a sharp, cutting movement. 'Let me see you take that dam down,

51

boys, 'cause we got some thirsty beef down yonder.'

They moved to obey, knowing that argument was futile. This time they had been caught out. This was Rocking-T's round. There was no use anyone else getting killed for nothing. Today Boxed-O ate crow — but there was always tomorrow. The men of Boxed-O cursed Andy Jacobs to high hell, but while they cursed they tore down the dam they had built. They toiled beneath a blazing sun and sweated, tearing raw hands on rough logs and blistering their skin on rock turned furnace-hot in the heat.

And as they worked they were always aware of Andy Jacobs and his ready gun, each of them knowing that he would use it without hesitation if the need arose. It only took a quick glance at the stiffening corpse of the man named Red to quell any thoughts of what would obviously be rash action.

While the larger part of his attention was focused on his four unwilling captives, Andy Jacobs let his mind consider the facts of what had just happened. The killing of Red bothered him only from the angle that he had most probably plunged Rocking-T into a war. The fact that he had killed a man didn't bother him at all. Red had made his play and had lost out, and that was as far as it went.

Jacobs' prime move from here would be to inform Jim what had happened. And knowing his employer like he did Jacobs knew that Jim Talman would back him up as far as it needed to go. It gave Jacobs some comfort. Even so he felt he had let Rocking-T down by precipitating this course of action.

When the dam was cleared and the new run-off blocked, Jacobs ordered the Boxed-O men to load their dead companion onto his horse so that they could take him back to Boxed-O headquarters. Before they did this Jacobs collected all the rifles out of the saddle-sheaths.

'Curly, you tell Olsen what went off

here,' Jacobs said. 'Make him see there's no point in taking it any further.'

Curly turned from where Red was being tied onto his horse. He stood with legs apart with his hands on his hips. 'I don't see it that way, Andy. Hell, Olsen's had his sights on Rocking-T for a damn long time, and he usually gets what he wants.'

'He won't get Rocking-T, or it's water.'

Curly swung up into his saddle. He sat, watching his companions move off. Before he gigged his own horse into motion he looked back at Andy Jacobs.

'Red was a good friend of mine, Andy,' he said. 'I won't forget you did for him.'

Jacobs shrugged his shoulders. 'It was a fair shoot-out. You figure to give me the same odds?'

A faint smile touched Curly's lips. 'Who knows, Andy, who knows?' He tipped his hat slightly. 'I'll see you, hombre. Watch your backtrail.'

Andy Jacobs climbed up to where he

could watch the line of riders descending the long, rocky slope that led down to Boxed-O range. He stayed where he was for over an hour. By then the riders were tiny specks far below him. Only then did he prepare to leave.

Collecting up the discarded weapons he bundled them under his arm. A swing of his boot put out the cookfire, sending the coffee pot rolling into the water. As the brew mixed with the water it spread a pale stain of brown that went with the flow, spilling through the run-off. Watching it Jacobs found his gaze being pulled to the dark, drying bloodstains where the man called Red had fallen. He wondered how much more blood, if any, would be spilled. It was something he couldn't answer. He hoped it would never need to be answered. It was a faint hope, he knew. Past experience had taught him that the desires and dreams, hates and emotions of men were things never to be reckoned with.

6

Unaware of what had taken place during his absence Jim Talman rode easy on his return to Rocking-T. With him rode the two hands he had hired while in town. Jim was pleased with his choice; both were seasoned cowhands who had been on the lookout for steady work for some time; when they'd heard of Jim Talman's call for riders they had ridden a long way to see him. Over a drink in the saloon Jim had assessed the pair and had made his decision. From the saloon Jim had returned to the store to collect Ruth's things, then he had rejoined his new hands and the three of them had ridden out of Garnett.

By the time they reached the creek the horses were eager to drink. Jim dismounted and moved about to stretch his legs.

'It's a fine piece of land, Mr Talman,'

Rem Callender said; he was a lean, sandy-haired man in his mid-thirties, his face tanned a deep brown from years of exposure to blazing sunlight and harsh, dry winds.

'None better,' Jim told him. He prodded a dry bunch of grass. 'Right now you're not seeing it at its best.'

'Drought.' Callender spat. 'Man, I seen enough of 'em to last me two lifetimes. Leastways, Mr Talman, you still got yourself some good water.'

'And we need it all,' Jim said as he mounted up again. Settled in the saddle he glanced at Callender. 'By the way, the name is Jim. Call me Mr Talman when I've got gray hair and a house full of grandchildren.'

Callender grinned, showing strong white teeth. 'I hope I'm with you that long.'

Josh Keel, Callender's partner, younger and darker, shaded his eyes as he spotted something moving towards them. 'Rider coming,' he said.

Jim recognised his foreman long

before Jacobs reached them. He felt a sudden tightness in him for something in the way Jacobs was riding spoke of trouble. It wasn't like Rocking-T's ramrod to push his horse so hard, and even more so in this kind of weather.

Dust boiled up in a stinging spray, coating men and horses as Jacobs reined in with near savagery, sawing his sweating horse around in a plunging semi-circle.

'Andy, you trying to ride the legs off that animal?'

Jacobs took his hat off and sleeved his face. 'I got to talk to you, and I mean now, Jim.' He glanced beyond Jim to where Rocking-T's new hands sat their mounts in watchful silence.

'Rem Callender, Josh Keel,' Jim said. 'Signed them on while I was in town.' Jacobs nodded to the pair as Jim told them, 'This is Andy Jacobs. He ramrods Rocking-T.'

Rem Callender inclined his head slightly. 'Heard of you,' he said. 'Good man by what the tale tells.'

'I hold my own,' Jacobs told him.

Callender nodded. 'Fair enough,' he said. He glanced at Jim. 'Josh and me better ride on if you got to talk, Jim.' He didn't wait for a reply, but spurred his horse away with Josh Keel following close.

'Good pair,' Jacobs remarked. He had dismounted and was on his knees beside the creek, swilling his neck and facc.

Jim got off his own horse and waited for Jacobs to speak. While he waited he rolled himself a cigarette.

'Jim, I had to kill a man,' Jacobs said straight out. He was facing Jim as he spoke and the pain was clear in his eyes.

'What happened, Andy?' Jim asked, and listened in silence as Jacobs told him, his anger growing with each word.

Jacobs finished his tale and trailed off into an awkward silence. Knowing him as he did, Jim began to realise just how hard Jacobs had been hit by this. Rocking-T's foreman would never let himself forget that he had most probably landed his outfit in the middle of the biggest trouble ever to cross its path.

'Andy, let's get one thing straight here and now,' Jim said. 'I'm damned sorry this had to happen, but we didn't start it, and I'm not going to dwell on it. You had to kill a man — but he knew what he was doing and you've got no cause to worry. When a man carries a gun and goes to use it, then he'd better be faster than the man he's going against. This fellow obviously thought he was, but you proved him wrong. You beat him fair and square, Andy. What we've got to do now is figure Olsen's next move.'

'If he's so short on water we haven't seen the last of him.'

Jim nodded. 'Then we'd better be ready.'

Tipping his hat back Jacobs raised his eyes to the distant hills. 'A couple of the boys up at the spring with loaded rifles?'

'It's a start,' Jim said. He glanced

across at Jacobs. 'It's ours, Andy. Nobody takes Rocking-T. Nobody.'

It took them a few short minutes to catch up with Callender and Keel. Jim told them the situation in a few short sentences, his eyes alert for their reaction, and when it came he was not disappointed.

'Are you asking if we want to ride out?' Callender inquired.

'I want you to know what you'll be facing if you stay on with Rocking-T,' Jim told him.

'We didn't expect we were going to be joining an old maids' tea-party, Mr Talman,' Josh Keel said abruptly.

Callender smiled dryly. 'Josh don't say a deal, but when he does it generally makes sense.' He drew rein on his restless horse. 'Hell, Jim, I ain't run from trouble in all my life, and when I sign for a brand it goes for the rough as well as the smooth.'

Jim nodded his thanks and swung his horse's head around, aiming for home. He gigged his mount forward, the others falling in behind.

About half the crew were at the ranch when Jim got back. Dust lay in a grey-white cloud above the corral as fresh mounts were exchanged for the worn-out ones that had been on the go since morning; men swore and sweated in the blazing heat as horses played up and refused to be roped and saddled. The heat was getting to men and animals alike. It was getting worse, not better, Jim thought as he dismounted. He tied his horse to the hitching-post and took Ruth's packages with him as he turned towards the house.

'Andy,' he called, and when his ramrod joined him he said, 'Get the boys together. Let them know what's happened. And pick a couple of handy riflemen for the first watch at the spring. I'll be with you in a while.'

Jacobs nodded. Jim watched him tramp across the dusty yard, calling out orders as he went, and he was glad he had the blocky, tough man on his side.

He went into the house, with the

realisation that he now had to tell Ruth what had happened, and what might follow. He didn't doubt that she'd stick by him, for whatever came to hand Ruth would be by his side every step of the way. He knew though that she would worry, and worry could hurt just as much as physical violence.

Ruth was in the kitchen making butter. She glanced up from her labours as he came in, ducking his head to avoid the top of the doorframe. She was struck, as she often was, by his likeness to his late father; like John Talman had been, Jim was a big man, tall, with the powerful but spare build of a born and bred cattleman; he had the hip-lean, wide-shouldered hardness of a lifelong horseman. Ruth liked to believe Jim was a handsome man, but in reflective moments she had to admit his features marked him as homely good-looking rather than handsome. But there was something in his strong face that lent him a maturity his years might not warrant.

As he paused in the doorway Ruth saw the worry etched deep in his eyes; he was trying to hide it, but his eyes gave him away, and Ruth knew him too well to be fooled. Wiping her hands on her apron she rounded the table and put her hand on his arm. 'Jim, what's happened?'

Jim put the packages on the table, then crossed to the stove. He poured a cup of coffee and sugared it.

Her voice edged with impatience, Ruth repeated her question. She stood before him, eyes fixed on him firmly, waiting for him to speak.

'Olsen moved against us this morning. He damned up the creek at the spring and turned it down his side of the hill.'

'He has our water?'

'He had,' Jim said. 'Andy found out what was going on. He got the drop on Olsen's men and made them tear the dam down so we got our water back.'

'That isn't all though, is it?' Ruth asked. 'Is it?'

Jim shook his head. 'One of Olsen's men tried to outshoot Andy. He didn't make it. Andy killed him.'

'Oh no. Jim, poor Andy.' Ruth fought back the panic that was threatening to rise. 'Is Andy all right?'

'He figures that if we get pulled into a range war it'll be his doing.'

'That's nonsense, Jim. What else could he have done if he was in danger of being shot himself? He must see that.'

'I told him the same.' Jim refilled his cup. 'But you know how he feels about the place. He'd do anything rather than be the cause of any trouble for Rocking-T.'

'Are we going to have trouble, Jim?'

Jim put his coffee down. The drink had somehow lost its taste.

'I think we are, Ruth,' he told her, and he suddenly knew it was the truth.

7

Philip Olsen stood motionless on the porch of Boxed-O's main house and watched as the body of the man called Red was carried away. Olsen's smoothly-handsome face was dark with barely-concealed anger. Though some of that anger was directed towards the man who had killed Red, the greater part was channelled in the direction of this abrupt and violent opposition to his first move of what was intended to be the complete takeover of Rocking-T. He had bided his time and had planned as close as he could. True, he had expected Rocking-T to fight back, but the way it had come had been a shock to him. It meant one thing to Philip Olsen — a direct rejection of his power, of his potential threat to Rocking-T's existence. It showed that Rocking-T was prepared to fight it out all the way, and if that was the case, Olsen decided, Jim Talman was going to find himself in the middle of hell on earth.

'Frank, come into the house,' Olsen called to his foreman, Frank Spode, then turned and went inside without waiting.

Spode hesitated momentarily, glancing at an upstairs window where he'd seen the lace-curtain move. He dragged his gaze away from the window and forced himself into the house, hat in hand. His boots made loud sounds on the hard, polished wood floor, and he became conscious of his dusty, sun-bleached clothing. Spode paused in the wide entrance-hall, wondering where Olsen had gone.

'In here, Frank.' Olsen stood in the doorway of the small room that served as his office.

As Spode turned to join him he saw movement at the head of the long stairway that led to the upper floor. He jerked his head that way, and saw Olsen's wife, Victorene, watching him.

She was wearing a thin white robe over her firm, young body and her thick, red-gold hair was loose about her shoulders. Spode threw a swift glance towards Olsen's study. The Boxed-O owner was pouring whisky into thick glasses. Spode put up a hand and waved Victorene away. Here and now was not the place nor the time. He swore under his breath. If his feelings for Victorene were not as strong as they really were she could soon become a damned nuisance. As it was they took a risk every time they met. The fact that they loved each other would amount to less than nothing if Olsen ever found out. Spode pushed his thoughts of Victorene to the back of his mind as he strode into Olsen's office, closing the door behind him. He suddenly realised there was sweat on his palms.

Olsen handed him a filled glass. 'Sit down, Frank.'

Perched on the edge of a hard-backed chair Spode toyed with his glass, waiting for his employer to speak.

Olsen took his time. He began to pace up and down behind his big oak desk, his own drink forgotten in his large, thick-fingered hand. Spode got the impression of a huge, caged animal sizing up the limitations of its prison. As Olsen moved the powerful muscles in his jaw worked violently; it was the giveaway sign of Olsen's agitation, and anyone who knew him thought wise to tread wary at this tell-tale sign. To incur Olsen's wrath was to dance with the very devil, for the man had a brutal, explosive temper when aroused.

Abruptly Olsen dropped into the leather-padded chair behind his desk and stared hard at Spode. 'I want every man to go fully armed and ready for action from here on in.'

Despite himself, Spode said, 'It figures.' He hadn't wanted to say too much at this point. But his feelings were strong, and he knew that it would have to come out before too long. The truth was that Frank Spode opposed Olsen's ideas. To his way of thinking

Boxed-O was big enough for any man. Olsen was just plain greedy. Spode had seen that greed grow over the past few years and the realisation had always left him with an uncomfortable feeling. Spode was a cattleman, not a landgrabber; his trade was ranching, not carrying a gun for hire. The pattern of life at Boxed-O had changed from that of a working-ranch to a heavily-armed camp of gun-handy roughriders. Spode had gotten heartily sick of it. He'd kept strictly to his own job of running the ranch, but the fact that he was foreman meant that he was involved in whatever Olsen decided to do. He tolerated it, but he was at the end of his patience. Spode knew that it was only Victorene who kept him at Boxed-O now. But if a range war was on the way he wanted nothing of it, and knew he had to get Victorene and himself out.

'You don't exactly sound enthusiastic,' Olsen said, and there was a hard edge to his voice.

Spode faced him squarely. 'If you

want it straight I'm not.' Now the time had come he found that the words came easy.

Olsen stiffened. The knuckles of the hand that held his glass went white with tension. 'You feel like explaining?'

'I'm a cattleman, Mr Olsen, not a gunfighter. I've worked for you as a cattleman but I won't work as a hired gun, or a man who has to mix with the kind of scum you're hiring these days.' He raised his glass and drained it. 'I don't figure it to bother you, but you carry the blame for Red being killed today. Hell, do you expect Jim Talman to hand Rocking-T over to you without a fight? What went off today is just what I expected. You've no legitimate quarrel with Talman.'

'You think not?' Olsen arched forward in his chair.

Spode pushed to his feet, surprised at his own calmness. He placed his empty glass on the desk. 'Mr Olsen, you're a greedy man. You figure that if you see something you want all you have to do is reach out and take it. Boxed-O is big enough for any man — but not you. Trouble with being greedy is that a man never knows when to stop.' Spode turned to go, then stopped. 'I figure Jim Talman to give you a fight you won't forget, and he might just beat you.'

Olsen's fury was suddenly plain to see in his eyes, in the set of his mouth. He came up out of his chair. 'Spode, you're fired. Collect your gear and get off Boxed-O. And stay off.'

'I aim to,' Spode told him. 'You can send my money to the bank in town.' He turned then and walked out of the room and out of the house. Crossing the yard he went into the bunkhouse and began to pack his belongings. Suddenly he wanted to be away from Boxed-O. Victorene was strong in his thoughts, but he would have to be patient and wait his chance to see her. Once she found out he'd left she would get word to him.

Philip Olsen was still in his office when Spode rode out a half-hour later.

He watched his ex-foreman go without a flicker of emotion on his face. His mind was already at work on deciding who to give Spode's job to.

Olsen spent some time alone with his thoughts and the decanter of whisky. When he finally emerged from the study he left the decanter empty. The whisky had done nothing to improve his disposition, for his anger had turned sour, leaving him sullen and bitter.

He made his way upstairs, slightly unsteady. He wasn't certain why he was going upstairs, and at the head of the stairs he paused before turning to the main bedroom. The door stood half open and Olsen was able to see into the room before he went in.

Victorene was seated before the ornate, gilded dressing-table, brushing her hair before the huge oval mirror. Olsen was struck, as always, by her strong womanly attractiveness, her unintentional sensuality. She was the kind of woman who drew the admiration of any man who laid eyes on her.

Olsen was unable to remember any man who hadn't been caught that way on seeing her for the first time.

It had been in a crowded ballroom, in Chicago, during his trip there to conclude a number of important negotiations; there had been prices to fix, delivery dates to agree on, and contracts to sign. When they had finally been signed Philip Olsen realised he was a made man. At the time he was also a tired man, and he had decided to stay on for a while. Rest and relaxation were what he needed. Chicago had provided both. He had allowed himself time to enjoy the bright lights and the nightlife of the city. His name and his connections opened doors for him and brought him a number of invitations. Olsen took to the dining out and the social mixing with ease. When the need arose he could be as charming and as pleasant as anyone. His name began to be recognised, so did his face, and he found he was constantly being bombarded with introductions to unattached young women. It dawned on him that he was on the marriage circuit. At first it amused him and he played along for the pleasure it brought him. Later, though, he began to consider the matter seriously. He realised that what he needed was a wife. A wife would complete his image, would help him socially if he chose carefully. He began to cast around for himself and almost before he knew it Victorene Clavell came into his life. The grand-daughter of a bank-president, she was beautiful and intelligent. She came into view one night at a civic ball at one of Chicago's largest hotels. Olsen saw her and could not forget her. In the moment of seeing her he realised that this was the woman for him. He decided he wanted her, and as with everything he wanted, he went straight after her. In the forthright, blunt way of a born Westerner, he beat a path to her door and made his intentions clear. To his surprise, and pleasure, Victorene turned out to be fully receptive to his advances. Within a month he had courted and married her, and when he left Chicago he took with him the new mistress of Boxed-O.

Once back among his own kind, however, Olsen slipped back into the old ways, the old habits, and Victorene, after the first flush of marriage, was left to assess her position. It soon became clear to her that things were not as romantic and wonderful as she had expected. She was not struck by the Western way of life. Nor did she particularly enjoy the changeable climate; it was either too hot or too cold, there never seemed to be any middle way. Olsen himself, she had found, was not all charm and politeness. Gone were the expensive clothes, the white gloves. Now he wore rough range clothes that smelt of horses and cattle and sweat. He often went about unshaven, grimy with dust, a huge gun strapped to his waist. Also, he was a clumsy, hard lover and Victorene dreaded nights when he would reach for her and pin her beneath his straining bulk. She longed for the times when he stayed out on the range with his men.

Then Frank Spodc made his appearance in her life. In essence he had been there all the time. As Olsen's foreman he was in the house often, and Victorene saw him round the ranch every day. At first she hardly paid him any attention, but there came the time when her loneliness made her reach out for some alternative companionship. Spode himself had been taken by her at first sight. The constant nearness of her, yet the unbridgeable distance, made his life a near misery. He began to hunger for Victorene Olsen in a way he'd never hungered for a woman before. He was more than surprised when she began to show a considerable interest in him. Life suddenly took on a pleasant change for him, though he knew he was treading a dangerous ground. But no amount of worrying thought could change his feelings for Victorene, and there came the time when he revealed just how he felt about her. She was flattered and almost desperately responsive; responsive in a way Spode never believed possible. Their meetings had to be planned with great care, in secret, and though neither of them liked it this way there was nothing they could do about it. Until they could come to some solution, they realised, they would have to put up with the situation as it was.

Olsen knew nothing of this, due to the discretion of his wife and her lover. She was still his wife, beautiful, and to him dutifully faithful, one of his prized possessions. But even he had become aware of a strained atmosphere when they were together. He had enough on his plate to contend with and Victorene, he realised, was becoming a liability, and a bore.

Standing now in the bedroom door he watched his wife speculatively. She was unaware of his presence as she slipped her robe from her shoulders and began rubbing scented lotion into the milk-white firmness of her upper body. Olsen moved on into the room, pushing the door shut behind him.

Victorene half-turned as the door clicked into place. Her eyes were wide with brief alarm, her cheeks hotly red under the smooth skin. Her gaze faltered when it met Olsen's hard stare and she lowered her eyes swiftly. Olsen dismissed this as nothing more than womanly shyness, for Victorene had a natural reluctance for exposing herself before him. This sometimes annoyed him, but he let it pass, contenting himself with her complete surrender once they were in bed and in the darkness.

He watched her now, a faint smile on his lips. Victorene had raised her arms to cover her breasts, her body trembling.

'Please don't look at me that way, Philip,' she said.

'Why in hell not? You're my wife aren't you?'

'It isn't that.'

Olsen belched noisily, the action leaving a sour taste in his mouth. 'No, and it isn't Chicago. For God's sake, Victorene, quit this damned virgin maiden act. It isn't as if you were a skinny, flat-chested baggage.'

'Oh, Philip,' she said, shocked.

'Hellfire!' Olsen grumbed, abruptly irritable; it was a combination of the whisky, which always took him this way, and the turn of events that had occurred within the past few hours. 'Damn it, Victorene, stop playing so coy. A man wants a woman who knows what she's got and how to use it, not a simpering female who daren't even show her husband the colour of her tits.'

Victorene gasped, her face colouring hotly. 'You disgusting animal,' she said. 'I won't take that from anyone, let alone you.' She was on her feet now, forgetting her nakedness in her anger.

'Talk about wanting a woman do you — well what about me? Ever since I came here I've been waiting for a real man to share my bed with.' Her voice rose. 'Do you hear? A real man, not a clumsy, fumbling pig like you.'

A fury rose in Olsen, born of pride and shame, for inside he knew her words were true, though he would never admit it, not even to himself in so many words. The fury swelled and grew, taking control of his thoughts and actions. He swung his big right hand up and hit Victorene across the face. Once, twice and then again.

Victorene stumbled away from him, the shock of pain in her eyes, on her face. The backs of her legs caught on the edge of the dressing-table and she sprawled across it, sending jars and bottles of cosmetics sliding over its polished surface. She remained where she was, her eyes challenging him to touch her again. Her face was blotched red where he had hit her and a thin line of blood dribbled across her lower lip.

'Pig! You call me a pig.' Olsen's voice was hard, anger still very close to the surface. 'Maybe to your refined way I am a pig. But remember what I own, what I've built. I might be an animal to you, but to everyone around here I'm a big man, a powerful man.'

He turned for the door, jerking it open with near savagery. He spun on his heel, his back ramrod straight.

'It appears, my dear,' he said in mock civility, 'that we have reached a turning-point in our relationship. Either we have been deceiving each other, or fooling each other all along. Whichever way it is things have come to a dead-end. Right now I have enough on my mind without adding this situation. Until I can make any decision affecting our future I suggest you stay out of my way.'

He dragged the door hard shut behind him, standing outside for some time, trying to clear his head. Victorene's outburst, the obvious distaste she held for him had come as a shock and a revelation. It was clear to him now that whatever feelings he'd ever had for her had been purely physical; her beauty, her projected sensuality had been what he had been attracted to — and it came to him that in all the time he had known her, never once had he said that he loved her.

As he began to descend the stairs he could hear Victorene's muffled sobs from behind the closed bedroom door. It did nothing to him, and by the time he reached the foot of the stairs Victorene was out of his thoughts altogether.

8

From where he stood Jim Talman was able to see clear down Boxed-O's side of the hill range. The vast sweep of land opened up below him, fanning out to all sides, an endless carpet of sun-browned grass.

Behind him, at a higher level, Andy Jacobs and two of Rocking-T's hands were setting up the chosen site where they would mount guard over the spring. Jim turned, glancing up to watch them for a minute. It gave him a cold, tight feeling seeing the preparations, for it was as near to war as any man could get short of joining the army. He had always known that a range war was possible, but this knowledge didn't make the reality any less grim. This was what his father had fought to forestall ever since he had created Rocking-T; John Talman had succeeded, and Jim felt he had failed his father on that score. But he'd had no choice, and if he was going to hold on to Rocking-T then he was going to have to be prepared to fight for it. He was reluctant to do so — but if Olsen put his back to the wall there would be a fight, for Jim had no intention of being the loser.

Moving off the rim Jim eased his way through fallen rock and scrubby undergrowth, then began the climb up the rocky facing of the outcropping that held the source of Rocking-T's water, the spring. From here a man had an unobstructed view down to Boxed-O range. It also meant that a man with a rifle would have a clear shot at anyone coming up the slope.

Jim slapped dust from his clothing as he completed his climb. It was late afternoon, but the heat still held, making the men who worked on the high rock listless, with nerves close to being rubbed raw. Jim realised it was a bad time for something like this to happen. Everyone would be jumpy enough and sun-frayed nerves were no help at all.

'We're about as set as we'll ever be, Jim,' Andy Jacobs told him.

'Maybe.' Jim cast his eyes around the improvised camp. 'Figure it this way, Andy. If they can't hit us here they can try somewhere else.'

'The water's what they want. What they need.'

'Olsen wants all of Rocking-T,' Jim said, and they all knew he was right.

Jacobs made a sound of annoyance. He pulled his hat off and scrubbed his hand through his hair. 'Why the hell don't we ride down and finish this now. Burn Olsen out, shoot him out.'

There was a heavy silence. Jacobs looked from face to face. His anger subsided as swiftly as it had risen. He shook his head, jamming his hat back on in frustration.

'I guess I've done enough shooting just of late,' he said.

Jim punched at his arm. 'You talk too

much,' he said. He turned to the two Rocking-T hands. 'Now take it easy. Keep your eyes open. One of you on watch all the time. Work it out between you. 'Come morning I'll have you relieved.'

'Fair enough, Jim,' a tall, thin puncher named Davies said.

His partner, a lean, moustache-wearing man called Saintly Jones, spat a stream of tobacco juice into the dust. 'Don't you fret none, Jim-boy. Any of Olsen's crew come anyways near here they'll soon forget about water.'

'Try not to push it, Saintly,' Jim said.

'Why, Jim-boy, as if I would,' Saintly told him solemnly, his bony face reverently deadpan. 'Now you go about your affairs an' don't worry.'

Jim smiled at the man dryly. He knew he could trust them not to start anything without thinking about it first. They were as much a part of Rocking-T as anyone and would tolerate no thought or deed that might harm the spread in any way.

A short time later Jim and Andy Jacobs were riding down the wooded slopes to the flatlands below. About midway to the bottom this section of hillside levelled out into a wide, oval-shaped meadow. There was grass here and a good growth of trees. The creek ran in from above, meandered across the meadow, then dropped beyond the far side to continue on its downward journey.

Rocking-T beef was already here, though only in small numbers as yet. Jim hoped his decision to gather the entire herd up here was the right one. At least the herd would be in one place, a lot easier to control, here in the confines of this high meadow. Any strikes at Rocking-T could easily be aimed at its herds, and a stampede was a sure way of scattering or destroying a ranch's stock. On the wide flatland the herd was openly vulnerable, but up here, penned in and guarded it might prove difficult for anyone to cause trouble. Jim knew that he could be just as wrong. Nothing was ever certain in life. He had learned that lesson a long time ago.

A pair of riders converged on the spot where Jim and Andy Jacobs had reined in. They were Rocking-T's new men, Rem Callender and Josh Keel. Dusty and sweating they were pitching in to the work as if they had been with Rocking-T for years.

'How's it going?' Jim asked.

Callender sleeved sweat from his face. 'Fair. But it sure is hot. Man, I seen droughts and I seen droughts, but this is the daddy of 'em all.'

'You said it, boy,' Jacobs agreed. He was rolling a cigarette.

'Still a few more hours before dark,' Jim observed. 'If we stick with it we should have well over half the beef up here for the night.'

'Still leaves a hell of a lot down below,' Jacobs told him.

Jim nodded. 'I know, Andy. All we can do is keep them bunched and ride herd on them.' He eased himself in the saddle. 'Let's hope Olsen doesn't decide on a night raid.'

'Yeah, let's hope he don't,' Jacobs remarked.

'Jim,' Callender asked, 'you want me and Josh should stick up here tonight?'

'Yes. You got grub?'

Keel patted a bulging flour sack slung behind his saddle. 'We got grub,' he said.

Jim smiled. 'Ride easy then.'

Callender raised a hand, then rode off with Keel close behind.

'Ready, Andy?' Jim asked and led the way across the meadow. They moved into the trees that marked the commencement of the downward fall of the hill. Dappled shadows criss-crossed men and horses as they entered the trees. Rough grass broke beneath the hooves of the horses. A stillness lay around them, but far below them could be heard the sounds of bawling cattle and the yells of the men driving them.

After a time they broke out of the trees onto a stretch of open hillside, an uneven, sun-dried lay of land. Just off to their left the first of a large bunch of cattle came into sight from out of a steepsided gully that was part of the well-worn trail up to the high meadow. Dust billowed up around the jostling animals as they pushed and bawled their way out of the mouth of the gully. A half dozen of the long-horned beasts broke away from the main bunch and headed towards where Jim and Andy Jacobs were riding.

Reining his horse around Jacobs took off after the breakaway bunch, gigging his mount into a hard gallop. The steers saw him coming and instantly took flight. Jim was about to go to his foreman's aid when he heard his name being called. Twisting in the saddle he saw a rider approach, one of his own men who had been chasing cattle up the gully.

'Glad I caught you, boss,' he said, reining in his sweating horse. He was a stockily-built, pale-eyed Dutchman named Jan Dorn, who went by the nickname of Dutchy. He was a stolid, humourless man with more patience than Jim had ever seen in any ten men put together.

'Anything wrong, Dutchy?' Jim asked, and found he was almost dreading the answer.

Dorn glanced across to where Andy Jacobs' stocky figure appeared and disappeared in the swirling dust that boiled up around him and the bunch of steers he was chasing.

'Down on the flat,' he said. 'We run into Sheriff Nolan. He is for the house he tell us.'

Jim had forgotten his invitation to Garnett's lawman. Nolan, never one to dally, must have decided to make his visit that very day. Maybe it was for the best, Jim thought. Nolan would have to know what was going on sooner or later and it might be better to talk to him out at Rocking-T, away from town.

'How long ago, Dutchy?'

'Not long. Maybe only a half hour, not less.'

Jim watched Jacobs for a minute. His foreman had the runaway cattle on the way back to the main bunch.

'Nobody say anything about our trouble, boss,' Dorn said. 'We think maybe is better you tell him. Is correct?'

'Thanks, Dutchy. I'll go after him. Tell Andy I'm riding on. He can stick with you boys and make a tally on how many head there are to be brought up.'

Dorn nodded and rode out to meet Jacobs. Waiting until he caught Jacobs' eye Jim raised a hand, then turned his horse downslope, making for the distant flatlands.

It came to him as he rode that this was the second time in one day that he would be reporting trouble to Ben Nolan. This time, though, he realised, there would be no brushing it aside. Jim wished he could rid himself of it so easily, but he knew there was no chance of that. His conflict with Olsen would have to be faced and fought all the way down the line.

9

After collecting their guns from Sheriff Nolan, and also a hard-delivered warning from Garnett's lawman, Dunc Howser and Cal Jarrett made their way down to the saloon. The pair were in need of consolation to their way of thinking. As with most of their kind they soon got to feeling sorry for themselves; it was the two of them against the world, and a hard world at that.

Slouching into the saloon the pair found an empty table. Howser lowered himself into a chair while Jarrett went to the bar for a bottle and a couple of glasses. Returning with them Jarrett dropped into a chair across from his partner. Pouring whisky into the glasses he eyed Howser's swollen lips.

'Figure you'll be able to drink all right?' he asked.

Howser scowled. He slammed his stained hat on to the tabletop. 'You talk too much,' he said, wincing at the pain he felt in speaking.

'What did I say?' Jarrett protested. 'Huh? What'd I say?'

Howser tossed off his drink, shuddering as the whisky burned his lips. 'Goddam!' He dabbed his mouth with a kerchief from his pocket.

'My chest pains me somethin' awful,' Jarrett murmured, more to himself than anyone else. He drank his own whisky and watched Howser tackling his second glass.

They were still nursing their wounds, and the whisky bottle, when the batwings swung open and two men came in. Howser glanced up and studied them. Eventually he recognised them. One was the cook's louse from over at Olsen's Boxed-O, the other was an old cowhand who was now relegated to general handyman around Olsen's spread. Both men made their way to the bar and ordered drinks. Even in his drink-hazed state Howser was able to realise that the pair were more than a little agitated. There was, he decided, something in the wind.

He soon found out what it was. The Boxed-O pair were plainly eager to tell the tale they were carrying, and after a couple of drinks they were giving it free rein to every ear in the place.

Dunc Howser was one who received the news with more than a passing interest. The plain fact that Jim Talman was on the spot made him smile. That Talman was up against Philip Olsen's Boxed-O added an extra twist. Boxed-O was the biggest spread in the territory, big enough and powerful enough to swamp Rocking-T and make it vanish from the face of the earth. Olsen had been after the Talman spread for a long time and now it looked as though he was making his grab. Howser could see a range war on the horizon, and it made for interesting thinking.

Reaching for the bottle Howser

emptied the remaining whisky into his glass. Jarrett was sitting watching him, his face morose, and Howser suddenly grinned.

'With Talman and Olsen at each other's throats this piece of country is going to liven up some.'

Jarrett's face soured even more. 'Range wars make a lot of trouble. Hell, Dunc, best thing for us is to get out now, before the thing blows wild.'

'Get out? Damn you, Cal, can't you see we got us a chance to make us some money out of this.'

'How?'

Howser's bloodshot eyes shone suddenly. 'I got me an idea. Just come to me.' He shoved to his feet suddenly, jamming his hat back on. 'Come on, Cal, get your butt off'n that seat.'

'Where we goin'?' Jarrett stumbled as the searing heat struck him as they left the saloon.

Howser grinned again. 'Tell you all about it on the way,' he said.

They mounted up and Howser led the way out of town. Jarrett was silent for some time, then he asked again, 'Dunc, where we goin'?'

Howser spat into the dust. 'Boxed-O, that's where we're goin'. We're goin' to see Olsen and he's goin' to give us a job.'

Jarrett's head jerked around, and his unshaven face was puzzled. 'Job? What kind of a job?'

'One you'll enjoy, Cal. You and me are goin' to get somebody out of Olsen's hair for good and all.'

'Who?'

'Figure it, Cal. Just figure who's standing between Olsen and Rocking-T. Somebody Olsen'll pay to have removed.'

Jarrett nodded in sudden understanding. He gave a low chuckle. 'Jim Talman.'

'You named it, boy.'

'You mean a gun job, Dunc?'

'Sure. Kill him.' Howser eyed his partner. 'You don't like the idea?'

Jarrett laughed. 'Hell, sure I like it.

Best damn idea you had in a coon's age.'

Shortly after leaving town the pair took the branch-trail that led towards Boxed-O, and they eventually rode past the stone marker that signified the beginning of Boxed-O rangeland.

It was well into the afternoon when they sighted the buildings of the Boxed-O headquarters. The place looked deserted. There were horses in the large corral, restless in the dusty heat. Apart from the animals no other living thing moved in the sun-bright ranch yard.

From where they sat their sweating mounts, Howser and Jarrett were able to see down onto the ranch complex and then beyond where, far to the north, a pall of dust filmed the air.

'Somebody moving beef,' Jarrett said, pointing towards the dust-cloud. He was sweating heavily about the face and neck, his dirty shirt clinging to him front and back.

'Means there won't be many folk

home,' Howser said. 'If Olsen's there that's all we need.'

They rode down slowly, crossing the yard to rein in before the huge house. Easing in the saddle they looked the place over.

Howser tipped his hat back. 'It's a hell of a place,' he said.

'You like to told the truth,' Jarrett agreed. 'Man, oh, man.'

Howser was preparing to dismount when the house's big main door opened and Philip Olsen stepped out. He came to the edge of the porch, his face hard and openly hostile.

'What do you tramps want? A handout?'

'Why no sir, Mr Olsen,' Howser said. 'We heard about your trouble with Rocking-T, and we come to offer our services.'

Olsen was amused. 'Tell me, Howser, just what can you offer me that I couldn't get done myself?'

Lowering his voice Howser leaned forward. 'If Jim Talman was out of the picture things might go easier for you. Huh?'

Olsen was silent for a moment as he considered the statement. Howser winked at Jarrett. Abruptly Olsen stepped off the porch and indicated that Howscr and Jarrctt should follow him. He led them over to the big main corral where they could talk without being overheard. Howser's intimation had interested Olsen strongly. He waited while they dismounted and tied their horses.

'All right,' he said, 'spit it out.'

Howser hunched his broad shoulders. 'You want Rocking-T pretty bad don't you, Mr Olsen?' He didn't wait for an answer. 'Jim Talman won't let it go without one hell of a fight. You'll probably win in the end, but I'd bet it'll cost you one way and another. Am I right?'

'So you've proved you can figure things out by yourself.' Olsen's voice became edged with impatience. 'Get to the point, man, I haven't got time to waste.'

Howser let the cold words pass over him, smiling easily. 'All right, Mr Olsen. It's this way. You give us the nod and we'll have Jim Talman being measured for a pine box before you know it.'

Jim Talman dead.

The thought settled well with Philip Olsen. Without Talman Rocking-T would go under with much less fight than if he were at its head. It was Talman who held the spread together. He was the source of Rocking-T's strength — take him away and Rocking-T would fall apart in no time.

Olsen glanced at Howser, then at Jarrett. Pay these two enough and they would kill anyone. Their price might be high, but it would be cheap compared to what a drawn-out range war could cost him in time, money and men.

'You keep me out of it,' he said.

'Easy done,' Howser said. 'All you got to do is to carry on as normal. Leave it to me and Cal.'

'And your price?'

A new light shone in Howser's eyes.

He scrubbed a big fist across his jaw. 'Three thousand apiece,' he said. 'Half now — half when the job's done.'

Olsen's face remained blank. 'Very well.' He paused. 'You wouldn't try a double-cross would you, Howser?'

'Run off as soon as we get our hands on the money?' Howser laughed. 'Hell no! I know how big you are. That's enough for me.'

'Meet me in town, at the livery, about noon tomorrow. I'll have your money.' Without further talk Olsen turned and retraced his steps to the house. He heard the men he'd hired to commit murder ride out, and he felt well satisfied with the transaction that had just taken place.

10

With the evening meal over, lamps were lit against the fast approaching darkness. Though the bright heat of day vanished with the setting of the sun the sudden blackness of night still held a sullen warmth that threatened to cling and stifle. Above the dark land the sky broke into pinpoints of light as stars appeared, and a silence fell over the wide, empty country, broken only by the feverish activity at Rocking-T headquarters.

Over coffee Jim and Ben Nolan got down to the talk they had avoided during the eating of Ruth's meal. While the meal had taken place they had tried to keep the atmosphere clear, but a brittle tension had developed and the light-hearted banter had finally died into uncomfortable silence. Ruth had sensed that the two men wanted to talk;

she cleared the table, then disappeared into the kitchen. Jim had passed Nolan a thin black cigar, filled his own pipe, and had sat back.

Ben Nolan lit his cigar, letting writhing smoke rise above his head. He glanced at Jim, his face suddenly taut. 'This can't go on, Jim,' he said. 'I'll have to try and stop it. Long as I wear this badge I can't let a thing like this go on.'

'I know, Ben,' Jim answered. 'But I've got to fight him. I won't let Rocking-T go.'

Nolan sighed. 'Hell, Jim, I'd figure you a quitter if you did. I'd do the same in your place.' He leaned forward. 'That's as far as I go, Jim. A man has a right to protect himself and his property, but that's as far as it goes. Any man who breaks the law will have me on his tail. And that applies to friend or otherwise. Understand that, Jim, here and now.'

Jim nodded. He knew Nolan well enough to realise that the lawman meant every word he said. Nolan would carry out his duty to the end, regardless of whether the lawbreaker was a close friend or a total stranger. When it came to applying the law Nolan gave nothing. He walked a thin line and never even thought of stepping to either side of it. Jim respected this in the man and wouldn't have it any other way.

'What do I do, Ben?' Jim asked. 'How do I settle this? It's doubtful I could talk Olsen out of it. This water problem is all the excuse he needs to justify anything he does. In his own eyes he's in the right.'

'Like hell he is.' Nolan pushed up out of his seat. He prowled restlessly about the room. 'Jim, you know as well as I do that it's going to be a long time before we've got any really effective law in this territory. Hell, I got no more chance of upholding complete obedience to the law than you have of becoming king of England. So it means that every man has to be his own law — but only up to a point. Olsen has already gone beyond that point. I'll go see him and make it clear how I stand. I don't figure he'll worry too much over that, but if he pushes me I'll push back. I may get my head shot off, but I figure that's a chance I get paid to take.'

'In effect, Ben, you're telling me I'm going to have to fight, one way or another.'

'Unless a miracle happens,' Nolan said. He smiled wryly. 'Maybe if I make convincing noises Olsen will decide to quit.'

'Ben, you give as much comfort as a pair of tight pants.'

A soft laugh came from Nolan's throat. He ran a big hand through his hair. 'You'll make it, Jim I know it. You're John Talman's son and I know the way the Talman's fight.'

'You make it sound easy.' Jim straightened out of his chair as Ruth came back into the room.

Eyeing the two men, who had fallen silent again, she let go an exasperated sigh. 'For a minute I thought I was alone,' she said. 'Do you have to shove the body under the table every time I come into the room? I know you're only trying to keep me from worrying, but I wish you wouldn't.'

Nolan grinned. 'Jim, if I had a girl like Ruth in back of me I'd take on the whole damn world.'

'I guess you're right,' Jim said. He put an arm around Ruth's waist. 'You figure we can whip Olsen, honey?'

'Yes, Jim, we can, and we will,' Ruth told him.

Stubbing out the remains of his cigar Nolan reached for his hat.

'Ruth, I want to thank you for having me over. Both your cooking and your company are things I look forward to. Don't let anyone ever tell you that a body is better off on their own. It just isn't so. Home and family are the only things worth while.'

Ruth put her hands on his shoulders and kissed him gently on the cheek. 'That was a lovely thing to say, Ben. Thank you. And remember that you're welcome here anytime. No need to let us know you're coming, just open the door and walk in. You hear?'

'I'll remember, Ruth.' Nolan glanced at Jim. 'Keep your eye on her, boy, else I'll hoist her behind my saddle one day and light out for Mexico.'

'Like that is it,' Jim grinned. 'Looks as if I'll have to keep my eyes on the pair of you.'

The sound of men and horses reached them from outside and Jim realised that time was getting on. He went to the old rolltop desk where he did his paper-work. From a drawer he took out a rolled gunrig and strapped it on. It had been some time since he'd worn the gun and the weight of it on his hip was strange to him. Turning he saw that both Ruth and Ben Nolan were watching him. Nolan showed no emotion; he knew what it was all about and the sight of the gun did nothing to him. For a moment Jim avoided Ruth's gaze. When he did raise his eyes he could plainly see the worry in her face, the sadness in her eyes.

'Ben, would you tell the boys it's time to ride,' Jim asked.

Nolan put his hat on, nodded slightly. 'Sure, Jim.' His tone was soft, understanding. He turned and went out, closing the door behind him.

Ruth brought Jim's hat to him. She gave him a smile that was on her lips but not in her eyes. 'Please be careful, Jim.'

'I intend to be. All we're doing tonight is to relieve the boys on guard out there. Expect me back come dawn.' Jim took her in his arms. 'Dicken will be around so you won't be alone.'

'It's not me I'm worried for,' Ruth told him. 'It's you.'

'I'll be all right. Don't fret. I'll be back before you know it.'

Ruth smiled gently. 'And women weep while men go to war,' she murmured.

'Where did you hear that one?'

'I think I read it in a book.'

'Too many women forgetting where

they should be,' Jim told her with mock gravity.

'And where is that?'

Jim smiled. 'In the kitchen, woman, among the pots and pans.'

'Jim Talman, at times you talk like an old-fashioned prude.'

Jim kissed her hard, and for a long time; after a while Ruth relaxed in his arms, responding with tantalizing eagerness. When Jim finally pulled away, reluctantly, he saw Ruth's flushed, bright-eyed face, and he almost said to hell with riding out.

'You want me to hang up my hat and quit right now?' he asked.

Smiling, Ruth pushed a stray lock of hair from her cheek. 'Out, Jim Talman, out.' She eased him to the door, opening it for him. 'Out,' she said again, then held him to her for a moment before he left her.

Ben Nolan and the rest of Jim's crew sat their horses in a pool of light from the open cook-shack door. Crossing the yard to join them Jim's light-heartedness left him as fast as the night-gloom enveloped him. He mounted up in silence and led the way out of the yard. Ruth had already gone back inside, closing the door of the house behind her and Jim didn't look back as he rode away from the ranch.

A full moon had risen, throwing soft, pale light onto the wide land. Riding was made easy and Jim and his crew reached the herd in fairly quick time. As soon as they began to come across the bunches of Rocking-T cattle Jim set his men on the job of gathering them. With the light as good as it was he'd decided that they might as well carry on with pushing the herd on up to the high meadow. Too many of his beeves were showing the effects of the prolonged drought, and he didn't want this to go too far. The grass up in the high meadow was plentiful as yet. The trees and the rising hills around it helped to protect the meadow, keeping the ground active and the grass growth regular and steady. Somehow Jim had to try to keep his herd up there and hope at the same time that the grass lasted.

Ben Nolan threw in his hand, helping Jim and his crew to get the bunched cattle on the move. Once the herd was set and on its way Nolan eased his horse over to where Jim was, sitting his own mount, silently watching the passing stream of steers.

'Long time since I did anything like this,' Nolan said. In the moonlight his face shone wet with sweat. He cuffed his hat back, spat the taste of dust from his mouth. He eased up on one hip as he glanced across at Jim. 'Man, I figure I'm getting too old for this kind of thing.'

Jim smiled. 'That'll be the day. Ben, when are you going to see Olsen?'

Nolan settled back in the leather. 'I figure to cut across and see him as soon as I can.'

'Tonight?'

'The sooner the better. I don't aim to let him get away with this any longer than I can help.'

'You want any help?'

'No, I'll do it my own way. It's my job and I'll do it myself.'

'Take care, Ben.'

Nolan nodded. 'Will do, Jim.'

The bright moon stayed with them as the herd moved snakelike across the pale land. Dust from their passing hung thick and milky-white in the hot night air, the heat pressing heavy and dry against the faces and bodies of the sweating riders.

Andy Jacobs rode out of the dust-fog, appearing like some phantom in the long white duster he wore when he was driving cattle. The flapping skirts of the coat hid his legs and billowed out from his body like a cloak.

'At least they ain't got much fight in 'em,' he said. 'Heat's got 'em beat.'

'I know how they feel,' Jim said. 'Makes for easy handling anyhow.'

Jacobs sleeved his wet face. He hooked one leg over the saddlehorn and fished out his makings. With expert judgement he filled a paper, rolled and sealed it. 'I'll ride on and let the boys know we're coming. Don't want 'em to start shooting us by mistake.'

'All right, Andy,' Jim agreed. 'I'll give the boys a hand here.'

'Mind if I ride along, Andy?' Ben Nolan asked. 'I'm heading over to Boxed-O, so I may as well start now. You mind, Jim?'

'Go ahead, Ben, and watch yourself. Olsen's one tricky feller.'

'That's why I'm calling unexpected,' Nolan said. 'Catch a man off guard and you've got the upper hand from the first.'

With a brief wave of his hand the lawman turned his horse after Andy Jacobs. They angled away from the herd, fading into the darkness.

Gathering his loose reins Jim gigged his own horse forward, concentrating on the swelling mass of the herd. Time merged with the darkness and there seemed to be little else save dust and heat and jostling steers. Jim lost track of the minutes passing by. He saw ahead of him, finally, the gently rising slopes of the foothills. Above them the main bulk of the hills rose darkly against the moonlit sky. Turning in his saddle, he watched the straggling line of cattle with dust-smarting eyes. Once they had the herd on the marked trail that led to the meadow things would be easier.

A sudden shout broke through the noise of the herd's passing. Jim saw a rider approaching. As the horseman got closer a sudden tightness gripped him. The man wasn't one of his crew. Jim's hand dropped to his gun. He didn't draw it, but sat waiting, his fingers just touching the butt of the weapon.

He recognised the rider with something of a shock. It was Frank Spode, Olsen's foreman. Suspicions flooded Jim's thoughts. What did Spode want? Whatever it was, it was bound to mean trouble for Rocking-T somewhere along the line.

Frank Spode threw a quick glance at Jim's herd, then looked back at Jim.

'I've come to give you a warning, Jim,' he said.

'About what?' Worry knawed at Jim's inside.

'Bunch of Olsen's riders are planning to stampede your herd tonight. They aim to scatter them to hell and gone.'

'When's this going to happen?'

'Any time now,' Spode said.

'How come you're telling me this, Frank?'

Spode rubbed his jaw. 'Me and Olsen don't see eye to eye on things any more. Look, Jim, I'm a cattleman, not a gunslinger. Olsen's after Rocking-T and he doesn't mind how he gets it. I just didn't like the idea of being part of that kind of deal. I told Olsen how I felt and where I stood. The outcome of that was Olsen firing me, but I'd already quit.'

'And the raid?'

'I overheard some of the crew talking about it just before I rode out. Seems Olsen had decided the raid would be a follow-up to the try at your water. He had it all fixed before him and me had our little talk. I don't think he really trusted me from the start.'

'I'm grateful for this, Frank.'

'No need. I knew your pa, and he was a good man. Square as hell. Man in the cattle game has enough trouble without bastards like Olsen around. What he aims to do is wrong in any man's book and I won't stand by and let it happen without trying to do something about it.'

Jim caught sight of one of his men riding by. It was Jan Dorn, and he wheeled his horse round at Jim's call.

'Pass the word, Dutchy,' Jim told him. 'We've got trouble coming. Boxed-O is going to make a try at our herd tonight.'

'What you want us to do?' Dorn asked.

'Two of the boys can stay down here. Keep the herd where it is. The rest of us will get on up to the high meadow.'

Dorn turned his horse and pounded off into the night.

'Frank, what are you going to do now

you've left Boxed-O?' Jim asked.

Spode lifted his wide shoulders. 'Haven't decided yet.'

'Leaving the territory?'

'No.' Spode hesitated. 'I got personal reasons for staying around for a while.'

Jim didn't pursue the question any further. It was obvious that Spode didn't want to say any more, and Jim wasn't one to pry. he was too grateful to the man to offend him any.

11

In a couple of minutes Jan Dorn had all but two of the crew gathered round Jim. They sat silent and grim-faced as he told them what was liable to happen. The Rocking-T hands were not of the gunhand breed as Olsen's riders were, but Jim knew that if and when trouble reared its head they would fight as hard as any.

'One thing,' Jim concluded. 'If we tangle with Olsen's crew up there we won't be playing for marbles. I won't have time to issue orders so if anybody shoots at you remember you've got guns too. So shoot back and we'll worry later. Understand?'

They nodded and murmured their agreement. Jim felt satisfied. He had a good bunch here and he hoped they would all come through unhurt.

'Lead out, Dutchy,' Jim said. 'I'll follow up.'

As the Rocking-T crew rode away Jim turned to Frank Spode. 'I don't expect you'll be riding with us?'

'No offence, Jim, but I don't want to get involved any further.'

Jim understood. 'That's all right, Frank. Thanks anyway.'

Jerking his horse round, Jim set it out after the rest of his crew. He caught up with them as they reached the well-defined trail that led up to the high meadow. Taking the lead Jim gigged his horse up the rough, dusty trail. The way became steeper as they went higher, the slope curving its way out of the swells and hollows of the hill.

They had been riding for some ten minutes when the first shot rolled its sound into the night. It was followed by a second and then a short, heavy volley that rattled and popped its echoes around the slopes of the dark hills.

Fear and anger surged up in Jim; fear for the safety of his men, and anger at what Olsen's men were doing. His emotions urged him on. Driving his heels in, Jim forced his horse on up the pale, moonlit trail. As he rode he reached down and yanked his rifle out of the boot. He cocked it one-handed and rode with it across his thighs.

The gunfire continued and the higher Jim got the louder it sounded. At times it was ragged, uneven, then maybe just one or two guns firing widely-spaced shots.

Reaching the place where the trail began to level Jim drew rein, bringing his labouring horse down to a slow walk. His crew, following close, did the same. They crested the final slope, coming into the meadow, knowing that once they did they would come into the view of the Boxed-O raiders.

'Jim, on the right.' Jan Dorn's voice came from close to Jim's side.

Jim's head snapped round, eyes searching the gloom. For a time he could see only the blending mass of trees and brush merging with the denser background shadows. And then he saw one of the shadows move. It fused into the shape of a horse and rider. Jim stiffened. Was it a Rocking-T rider? Or was it a raider from Boxed-O? He got his answer moments later when the rider wheeled his horse, plunging it back through the brush.

'Comin' up the trail! Rocking-T!' The rider's warning rang loud and clear to every ear. And on the heels of his shout came the crack of a rifle.

Jim saw the yellow blossom of flame from the weapon and braced himself instinctively. His own rifle was coming up then, his finger squeezing the trigger. He felt the gun jerk as it fired, gripped his horse with his knees as the animal flinched from the muzzle blast. Jim knew he'd missed and swore softly as he levered another round into the breech.

The whole night lit up with the glare and flash of criss-crossing gunfire. The noise was deafening. Men yelled and swore. Horses squealed in terror.

Out of his saddle Jim found himself down behind an old and rotten tree trunk, with Jan Dorn beside him. The Dutchman, calm as ever, aimed and fired his rifle with mechanical precision. The only relaxing of his patience was a steady, almost inaudible stream of words in his native tongue.

The Boxed-O raiders had apparently decided to bunch together, for their entire outlay of gunfire originated from one area. Jim made it out as a jagged outcropping of eroded rock, overgrown with tangled brush, and it only took him a couple of minutes to realise that the way things were, the only thing that was going to happen was that both sides were about to use up a lot of firepower.

He found himself wondering how Rem Callender and Josh Keel were faring. He didn't doubt their ability to defend themselves, but until he knew for sure how they were he realised he would never settle. His thoughts were rudely interrupted as a rifle slug hit the tree he was sheltering behind. Rotten wood exploded dustily above his head, showering him with slivers and chunks. Some Boxed-O rifleman was ranging in close — too close, Jim realised, as another slug hit the same spot. Bringing his own weapon up Jim returned fire, sighting in on the distant muzzle flash.

Off to his left the brush rattled and cracked. Jim spun in that direction, his rifle ready. As his eyes adjusted to the gloom he saw a tall, slim figure easing out of the waist-high undergrowth. A second man was close behind, and Jim breathed easier as he became recognisable.

'Man, you really make a feller earn his pay,' Rem Callender said. He eased himself down deside Jim, thumbing his hat back. There was a faint smile on his face and he seemed to be enjoying himself.

'How'd it start?' Jim asked.

'They come over the hill trying to make like Indians,' Callender said. 'Only they made more noise than a rock in a rain-barrel. Josh an' me gave them a warning which, naturally, they ignored. So we let 'em have a couple of shots to show we meant it. After that things got a mite noisier. When you arrived we figured we might as well join you.'

'You see anything of Andy and Ben Nolan?'

Callender shook his head. 'They around here?'

'They rode up some time ahead of us. Andy was going to see if you were making out all right, and Ben was carrying on over to Boxed-O to have a talk with Olsen.'

'Well they never got to us.' Callender lost his smile. 'Hope they didn't get caught out in the open somewhere. Those Boxed-O boys have been shooting at every damn thing that moves.'

Before Jim could reply he heard a shout of alarm. He turned, crouched low, and moved along the line of men until he reached the one who had called.

'Hank, you see something?'

The man shook his head. 'Felt somethin'. Ground's shakin', Jim, I can feel it.' He was an old-time Rocking-T puncher, a grizzled, leather-faced man who had lived in and ridden this country as far back as when the Indians were about. He was tracker, scout, hunter, and a lot besides. He was seldom wrong and nearly always made his decisions on an age-old instinct. He cocked his head a little now as he palmed the ground again. His sharp eyes were hard as he looked at Jim. 'It's the herd, Jim. They's stampeding the herd. Boy, we'd better get the hell out of here, else we'll all end up as close to mother-earth as a man can get without being buried under it.'

Stampede. Shock immobilised Jim for a couple of seconds. In his mind he suddenly saw that huge herd on the run. He'd seen two stampedes in his time, and both had left him numb, overcome by the sheer destructive might that the normally placid steers could achieve in the collective strength of a stampede. The combined bulk and weight of countless bodies driven to a blind, panic-filled run could render men and horses helpless, could crush and destroy them in passing. He had seen wagons overturned and even buildings demolished.

Hank's voice reached Jim again. 'Jim, boy, you hear me?'

Realisation brought Jim out of it. 'I hear you, Hank,' he said. He began to move along the line of men. 'All right, boys, let's go. Move out fast. We got a runaway herd coming our way. Get to the high ground, and don't waste time. Move out.'

The Rocking-T crew began to pull away from their firing positions, grabbing the dangling reins of their wide-eyed, nervous horses.

Above the fading gunfire from the Boxed-O crew there now came a new sound. Not one man had to be told what that sound was. The low, thundering rumble, rising with every passing second, heralded the imminent approach of the stampeding herd. A faint tremor passed through the very ground, a rippling vibration that a man could feel through his boots.

'Move out, Rem,' Jim said to Callender. He saw the man nod and ease away, Keel close by.

The thunder of the fast-approaching herd filled the night. Jim noticed, too, that the Boxed-O gunfire had ceased altogether now. Before he moved off himself he turned to look back across the meadow, and he saw the herd coming out of the darkness. To Jim it was a bobbing, swelling dark mass, but it was enough to tell him that every steer that had been driven up to the meadow was there. While he was still fairly safe yet, a cold knot of tension grew in his stomach. There was little anyone could do to stop that crazed mass of running beef. Down on the flat, with plenty of open space, a crew of good men might slow and turn a running herd. But not up here. Not on this treacherous, dark slope of the hills where a man had his hands full watching out for natural hazards.

Jim turned to follow his crew, hauling his horse close behind him as he pushed through heavy brush that snagged at his clothing. He could see the rising shale slope ahead of him where his men were sweating and straining in their attempt to get their own fidgety animals to safety. A hail of stones and dust showered Jim as he started up the slope. His boots sank ankle deep in the soft shale and his horse baulked a couple of times, sinking back on its hind-quarters and rolling its eyes at Jim; there was nothing faster on earth than a horse for picking up the scent of fear; just let the atmosphere heighten and a horse would be fiddle-string tight in seconds. Jim hauled on the reins, struggling to keep his balance at the same time. He almost lost the horse, but the animal gave a sudden upward lunge that threw it forward and it crested the slope with

Jim still hanging onto the reins.

Below, where the Rocking-T crew had been only minutes before the earth was black with the heaving mass of cattle. Running wild and blind, the beasts smashed their way over rocks and through brush. The air was thick with dust and heavy with the rumbling, bawling noise of their passing.

Watching the seething flood of living beef pound its way into the night, Jim felt a clammy coldness dampen his skin. That had been as close as it ever needed to be. He felt a little weak, but he felt even greater the feeling of relief. Above the responsibility of running the ranch and its affairs was the responsibility he held for the lives and safety of the men who worked for him. Jim's father had held this to be of great importance and he had drummed this into Jim every chance he got. The full meaning of his position had never fully revealed itself until right now, and Jim found himself prepared for it.

He stood and watched the herd pass

by. Not until the tailend of the stampede had vanished down the gully did he turn to his crew.

'Anybody hurt?' was his first question.

From somewhere a voice said, 'I cut mah finger somethin' awful. They's blood all over.'

A general round of laughter greeted the complaint, and Jan Dorn's voice broke through. 'Is not blood, Cotton, is only some of that redeye you drink all time.'

Jim grinned as more laughter filled the air. He pulled his horse close and swung into the saddle. 'While you're all feeling so frisky, how about going down and seeing if we can pick up any of those Boxed-O trespassers?'

Men swung into saddles, checking handguns and rifles. The old puncher, Hank, pulled a wad of tobacco from his pocket and bit off a chunk. 'Let's get em', Jim.'

Rem Callender thumbed a final shell into his rifle. 'Josh and me can pick our horses up when we get down. We'll go on ahead, Jim.'

Jim nodded. He reined about and urged his horse on down the slope, letting the animal pick its own way. His crew strung out alongside of him, every man primed for action.

With the noise of the herd now far-gone, the night was quiet again. Had Boxed-O gone? It would have been an easy thing for them to have slipped away during the stampede. Jim found he was hoping they had on the one hand, for this would avoid any violent conflict, yet he felt that he had all the right in the world to strike back at the invaders. He found his emotions mixed, leaving him more than a little confused, and he had to realise finally that the only way to play this out was to take things as they came and to act accordingly.

12

Reaching the edge of the meadow Jim called a halt. He passed the order for his men to fan out, to cover as much ground as possible as they advanced. Riding forward in a long line abreast, the Rocking-T crew moved out across the silent, moon-dappled meadow.

It took only a minute for Jim to realise that Boxed-O had gone. Their aim tonight had only been to scatter Rocking-T's herd. This they had done, and that was enough for them this time. A running fight had not been on their minds.

Once again Jim brought his crew to a halt. He sat listening to the night, his ears straining to catch any sound. He heard nothing. And he realised that there was nothing to hear. Then, as he prepared to give the order to move out, he caught the faintest whisper of sound sifting gently across the meadow. Puzzled he leaned forward in the saddle and his eyes caught the soft sway of movement that was rippling across the meadow grass. Jim realised that what he had heard was the sound of a breeze blowing through the meadow, and then he could feel it cutting through his shirt and chilling his sweat-damp body. it was a cold breeze, coming in over the hills from the far north.

A horse brushed in close to Jim's and he glanced round. Jan Dorn, his broad face taut and thrust forward, was tasting the air. He nodded in satisfaction. 'You feel her, Jim,' he said, 'you feel her?'

'It's for rain, Jim, boy,' came the voice of the old puncher, Hank. 'No other wind like it. Man, it's goin' to rain like hell let loose.'

'I hope you're right,' Jim said. He raised his eyes to the sky and saw cloud scudding in from the north. Maybe Hank was right, he thought. He squared round in his saddle, faced his men. 'Move out, boys, but take it slow and easy. It looks like Boxed-O has gone home, only let's tread careful till we make sure.'

As he led his crew out again Jim saw Rem Callender moving forward on foot. Callender seemed to have spotted something. He stepped out into the open, rifle at the ready, moving smooth and fast. And then he was crouching, kneeling over something that lay in the long grass.

'Jim, over here.' Callender's voice was brittle, urgent.

Urging his horse forward Jim rode out across the meadow. Reaching Callender he swung out of the saddle.

For a few seconds Jim wasn't sure he was seeing the truth, but the illusion didn't stay with him long. He realised bitterly that he was facing cold hard fact.

Andy Jacobs and Ben Nolan lay close together in the trampled grass. A few yards beyond lay the humped shape of a downed horse. A hot sickness welled up in Jim as he dropped to his knees. He threw an empty glance at Callender.

'They're in a bad way, Jim. Looks like the stampede caught 'em head on.'

Jim bent over Andy Jacobs, gently raising his head. He tried not to look at the torn, bloody mess that was Jacobs' body. The white duster was in tatters and red with blood. 'Andy? Andy, you hear me?'

Jacobs' eyes opened slowly and he stared up at Jim. He seemed to be trying to bring his eyes into focus.

'I walked right into this one, Jim,' he said. Speaking was an effort, obviously painful. A trickle of blood appeared at the corner of his mouth, running down his chin.

'Just hold on, Andy, we'll get you home,' Jim told him. 'Just hold on.'

'I'll try, boy,' Jacobs said, 'but don't set your heart on me getting there. God, Jim, but I hurt.' He fell to coughing then, blood spilling from his slack mouth. He raised one of his shattered hands and clutched at Jim's arm. His body arched convulsively, his face twisting in sudden, silent agony. He sought Jim's face again with his eyes. 'Don't let it go, Jim. Don't let the bastard take it. You hear me, Jim? Jim, you there?' His eyes rolled upwards, a shuddering breath escaped him and he died before Jim could say a word.

Jim stayed where he was, cradling Jacobs' body in his arms. It was a hard thing to accept. Andy Jacobs gone. A part of Rocking-T impossible to replace. For Jim Talman it was a heavy blow, and right then he felt lost and completely alone. Suddenly he felt weary and cold.

The Rocking-T crew gathered round in silence. Jacobs' death was a shock for them all, and every man there had lost something. Jacobs had been a tough, uncompromising ramrod, hard when it mattered, but he'd been a friend to every Rocking-T rider and none of them would ever forget that.

Jan Dorn, his hat in his big hands, said, 'We take Andy home, Jim.' When

Jim didn't answer the Dutchman knelt beside him, a firm hand on Jim's shoulder. 'Is better we take him home, Jim. Is better for us all.'

'He's right, Jim,' Rem Callender said. 'Sheriff needs doctoring. He's banged up pretty bad.'

Awareness came back into Jim's eyes. He'd forgotten about Ben Nolan. A slow anger began to smolder in him. Olsen had a lot to answer for, by God, and answer he would.

Horses were brought up and willing hands helped to put the unconscious Nolan onto one, with a man in the saddle to keep him there. Andy Jacobs' body was placed on another and somebody covered him with a blanket.

Jim called Jan Dorn to him. 'Dutchy, ride for town. Find Doc Baily and get him out to Rocking-T.'

Dorn nodded and swung into the saddle. He reined his horse about and thundered off into the night.

'Rem, you and Josh ride up to the spring. See if the boys are all right.'

'Will do, Jim. You want us to take over from them?'

Jim nodded. 'Do that, Rem.'

As Callender and Keel mounted up and rode out, Jim and the rest of the Rocking-T crew moved out and began the ride back home. For once the general banter and laughter was missing. A silence lay over the crew, a quietness that would be with them for a long time.

They reached the gully that marked their trail to the foot of the hills. The earth was torn and churned by the recent passing of the stampeding herd. A number of mutilated carcases showed where cattle had stumbled, fallen and had been overwhelmed by the mass of the herd.

As they made their way down the gully, riding slowly over the treacherous ground, it began to rain. It was faint at first, then the few drops turned to many and the skies opened suddenly. Within minutes they were riding through a torrential downpour, a heavy, almost solid sheet of water that tumbled out of a sky turned ugly and black.

Jim turned his face to the darkened sky. Wide, swollen clouds filled the air, sullen and angry looking. There was no mistaking their shape. They were stormclouds, of the kind that meant rain and then more rain. Things had gone from one extreme to the other, he reflected. First drought and now the distinct possibility of everything being flooded by a prolonged spell of rain. Jim hunched his shoulders against the chill of the rain and the clammy cling of his soaked shirt. Nothing ever really changed, he thought, all that happened was that you changed one set of problems for another.

Behind him his crew rode in dejected silence, bodies held rigid against the cold and wet. Their thoughts were as black and sombre as the sky above them, and more than one of them held thoughts of killing in their minds.

Some way beyond them the Rocking-T creek was beginning to fill. The rain sluiced down out of the heights, soaking the ground, then finding its natural way to the winding stream. The water level rose swiftly, breaching the banks as it splashed downstream. Reaching bottom it foamed its way across the shadowed range.

The drought was over, but the threatening violence and anger-heat remained as strong as ever. For a short time things might simmer, appear to cool down, and then the fuse would spark into life again. It had to come. It was as natural as day following night and just as unavoidable.

13

It was still raining the next morning when they buried Andy Jacobs. At the rear of the house, some way up a long, gentle slope where a few trees grew, the man who had given his life for Rocking-T was laid beside his former employer John Talman and Talman's wife.

Every Rocking-T rider who wasn't out on the range at the time was beside the grave, bare heads bowed as Jim read from the worn old Bible that had belonged to his father. Ruth was there too, standing beside her father, Garnett's doctor, Nathan Baily.

The day was cold and grey, the sky showing no sign of clearing. Heavy clouds showed in abundance and the rain fell steadily, soaking everything and everybody.

Jim closed the Bible and raised his

head. He'd said a lot, but he knew inside that there wasn't enough time left in all their lives to say a complete thank you to Andy Jacobs. He turned his head to look at Ruth. Her face was wet from the rain — and from the tears that ran freely from her eyes.

'Let's go inside,' Jim said quietly. He took Ruth's arm and they went towards the house.

With the door closed against the rain they removed the shiny black slickers they'd worn. Doc Baily excused himself and went to look in on Ben Nolan. Since he'd arrived the night before Baily had hardly been away from Nolan's side.

Nolan himself was still unconscious. He'd suffered a broken leg and a number of broken ribs, plus a mass of cuts and bruises that had left him in a bad way. Garnett's lawman was going to be out of action for some time. What law there had been was now out of the way. If full-scale war broke out now there was no law to stop it

— unless it was gunlaw.

For Jim this was one more problem to add to the many he already carried. He was deeply concerned about Nolan's health; Ben Nolan was tough, but he'd been hurt badly. Someone would pay for what had happened last night. He'd lost one close friend in Andy Jacobs, and that burned like a raw, fresh brand. Above the hurt he felt Jim had another reason for wanting vengeance. Doc Baily had come to Jim the night before, after he had completed his examination on Andy Jacobs. The doctor had placed two small objects in Jim's hand, and had said softly, 'I dug them out of Andy just now, Jim.'

Long seconds had passed as Jim had stared at the two .44–40 calibre lead slugs in his hand. A knot of coldness filled his stomach as realisation of what they meant grew on him. Doc Baily had made a low sound in his throat. He had removed the glasses he wore to clean the lens. 'They were in his back, Jim,' he'd said.

The words were still strong in Jim's thoughts as he put the Bible away in the old rolltop desk. For a moment he stood there, momentarily at a loss. Events had taken turns that had left him a little stunned. He knew he had to snap out of it, but for the moment he was feeling the full weight of it all.

'Jim, come and have a cup of coffee.' Ruth's voice, behind him, was gentle but firm.

He turned and took the coffee she offered. It was hot and sweet and tasted like coffee had never tasted before.

'Are you going over to talk to Olsen?' Ruth asked.

'I've got to,' he told her. 'I don't know if it'll do any good but I've got to try.'

Ruth came to him and he held her close.

'Jim, I don't want you to end up like Ben — or Andy.'

'Nothing's going to happen to me,' he said.

'Oh, Jim, why do things like this have to happen?'

'Because some men are never content with what they've got. They always figure the next man's grass is greener than their own.'

'But it just isn't fair, Jim. Too much has gone into Rocking-T. Olsen has no right to it.'

Jim smiled gently. Women never complicated things, he thought. To them life was all black and white, with no intermediate shades.

'I agree, honey, and anyway he isn't going to get Rocking-T. And don't you let yourself forget it.'

From the back of the house Jim heard Doc Baily calling him. With Ruth close behind he went through to the bedroom where they'd put Ben Nolan. Doc Baily met them at the door, a tired smile on his face.

'He's awake,' he told them, 'and he wants to see you.'

'How is he?'

Baily straightened his drooping glasses.

'He's hurt bad, but he'll mend. It's going to take some time though. He'll need tending, and watching.'

'He'll be looked after,' Ruth said. 'I'll see to that, dad.'

Jim glanced at her, seeing the determined gleam in her eyes. She'd set her mind and he knew how stubborn she could be. Not that he had any arguments on this subject. If Ruth hadn't made the suggestion he would have made it himself.

They went into the bedroom and saw with relief that Nolan was not only awake, he was sitting up. Bandages swathed his body from the waist up and his broken leg was braced in wood splints. Even his face, though it was not bandaged, showed the marks of his injuries. Nolan, realising he had visitors, raised his head and managed a painful smile.

'How you feeling, Ben? Jim asked.

'Like I never want to feel again,' Nolan said. He glanced at Ruth. 'I said I'd be visiting again.'

Ruth sat on the edge of the bed. She tried to smile, but too much had happened and people she loved had been hurt. Tears flooded her eyes and she lowered her head.

'Lord, Jim, I'm sorry about Andy,' Nolan said.

'It's hit us all pretty hard.' Jim hesitated. 'Ben, did you see who did it to Andy?'

'I saw it up to where the herd hit us. After that things got rough. We'd got halfway across the meadow when all hell broke loose. Guns started going off, then the herd started to run. Andy and me figured it was another Boxed-O raid and we decided to see what we could do. Trouble was, we were right in the middle of it all. Andy said best thing we could do was to get to high ground. I remember we reined about, then I heard a yell and a couple of shots. I turned and saw Andy keel over and fall. I got down to help him, but the herd was too close. It hit us before we could move. I got a clout on the head and passed out.'

An awkward silence lay over them for a time. Jim knew what was going through all their minds, and he had a question that couldn't wait.

'Ben, did you see who shot Andy?'

Nolan raised his eyes from Ruth's motionless figure. He passed a weary hand over his face. 'When I heard the shots and turned I saw a rider heading away from us. He had a gun in his hand.'

'Who, Ben?'

'Curly Browning.'

'It figures,' Jim said. 'It was Curly who had words at the spring when Andy shot Olsen's rider. He said he'd settle with Andy.'

'But in the back, Jim?' Baily protested.

'We all live by different rules, doc,' Jim told him. 'Backshooters figure their way is the surest, and the safest — for them. If you're out to kill a man why do it in a way that gives him a chance to kill you?'

'Jim, what are you figuring to do about Curly?' Nolan's voice was friendly, but it was Garnett's law that was asking the question.

'I'm not going gunning for him if that's what you mean.'

'Glad to hear it, boy, 'cause I wouldn't want to have to arrest you.'

Ruth's head came up, her eyes flashing. For a moment it seemed she was about to let go at Nolan. Then she calmed and her taut body relaxed. She knew as well as Jim that there was only one set of laws, and a man was either on one side or the other.

'I think that's all for now,' Baily told them. 'Ben, here, needs rest. Plenty of rest. You two move out of here. Go on.'

'Jim,' Nolan said, 'you watch yourself. Olsen's got the bit in his teeth now. He's going to keep kicking.'

'He may get a surprise when Rocking-T kicks back.'

Nolan smiled and lay back.

Before he left the house Jim made sure he was carrying fully-loaded

151

weapons. He was hoping to keep his visit to Boxed-O a peaceful one, but there was no guarantee that was how it would turn out.

Ruth's goodbye was light, but it was strained.

Crossing the yard, ankle-deep in mud now, a far cry from yesterday's dust, Jim went into the bunkhouse. The big iron stove had been lit and the place was warm and steamy from drying clothing. Jan Dorn joined him, his square face set and expressionless.

'What is to be done for today, Jim?' he asked.

'Just gather the herd and make a tally. See how many we lost last night.' Dorn nodded, and Jim, watching him, knew he'd been right in giving him the job of foreman. Dorn had been with Rocking-T for a long time. He was tough, solid, dependable. He would take orders without question, but Jim knew that he could use his head if the need arose. 'Jan,' he added, 'just keep the boys on their toes. Olsen might strike again, anywhere. I don't want any more Rocking-T casualties.'

'I understand, Jim.' Dorn reached for his coat. 'How is sheriff?'

'Awake. He'll be in bed for some time, but he'll mend.'

'Is nasty this, Jim,' Dorn said. He began to pull on his coat. 'What happens about Andy?'

'It gets settled, Jan, but the right way. No shot in the back.'

Dorn fastened his coat tight. 'I tell the boys. They will understand. You ride with us today?'

'No, I'm going to Boxed-O for a talk with Olsen.'

'Is wise?'

'Hell, Jan, what's wise and what isn't just now? I've got to give it a try.'

'Sure, Jim, is right way.'

'I hope so,' Jim told him. He fastened his slicker across his throat as he left the bunkhouse, made his way to the stable. Clinging mud made his boots heavy. The rain continued to fall from a lead grey sky. Swollen cloudbanks warned that the rain was settling in for a seemingly long stay. Jim wondered just how long it would last. The drought was over and now it seemed as if the next problem would be an over-abundance of water.

Jim saddled up and rode out of the yard, turning his horse across country. He would cross the hills that separated his range from that of Olsen's, and then make his way across Boxed-O to the opposing headquarters.

He rode at a steady pace, keeping his horse away from soft ground as much as possible. The rain had turned the land sodden and water had gathered in every hollow. The grass would start to grow through soon, Jim realised, as long as the rain didn't wash the very roots out of the soil.

He saw odd bunches of Rocking-T beef here and there as he rode. The beasts were crowding together in collective misery as the rain sluiced down on their glistening hides. Twice he reined in and dismounted as he came across steers that lay motionless on the ground. Both times he found dead beef. Each steer bore extensive wounds, obviously received during the stampede of the previous night. The question in his mind was how many Rocking-T beeves were there like this?

Reaching the foothills he urged his horse up the wet slopes. The creek lay close on his right, the stream full to overflowing, water surging and roiling its way across the land.

The higher he got the rougher the ride became. Jim tired of dismounting in the end and eventually stayed on foot, leading his horse. Once he reached the tree-line the way became a little easier. Beneath the trees the ground was somewhat firmer. The overhead tangle of branches held back some of the rain. Here it was dim and shadowy, the air heavy with the damp smell of the trees, the musk of tree-mold and woodrot.

Breaking out from the trees Jim came upon the place where Callender and

Keel were keeping their vigil over the spring. He was below them yet, but he could see the jutting rock-formation that concealed their camp.

'Hello the camp,' he called, warning them of his approach.

Off to his left he heard movement. Rem Callender stepped out of the brush. He wore a dull, mud-coloured slicker and held a rifle. Beneath his dripping hatbrim his face was dark with beard-stubble.

'Heard you coming,' he said.

'Glad I'm a friend,' Jim smiled. 'I figured I'd crept up without you noticing.'

Callender grinned briefly, and Jim realised just how good the man was.

They moved on up to the campsite. Jim put his horse with the two already there. Callender was on his heels by a small fire built under a jutting over-hang. Jim saw bedrolls and personal gear spread out on the dry rock. He joined Callender and gratefully shucked his slicker.

'You want coffee?'

Jim nodded and Callender handed him a steaming tin mug of black brew.

'Where's Josh?'

Callender gave a vague wave of his hand. 'He's out there somewhere. You won't see him less he wants you to.'

Drinking his coffee Jim accepted the thin cigar Callender offered him and lit up.

Callender tipped his hat back. 'Damn shame about Andy. Man like him shouldn't go that way. Not shot in the back.'

'It won't be forgotten.'

'You know who done it?'

'Ben was able to talk this morning. Just after Andy was downed, Ben says he saw a feller called Curly Browning riding off with a gun in his hand. He didn't see him do it, but it fits the picture. Curly said he'd get Andy for the killing of Red.'

Callender studied his coffee mug. 'Curly Browning. Hell, I know him. He's a bad hombre. Had him in my

157

sights once during a war way over at Kittyhawk. My hammer hit a dud shell.'

'Sounds like Olsen has hired himself a bunch of professionals.'

'If they're all like Curly Browning, then he has.' Callender watched the rain for a while. 'Jim, can I give you a word of advice?'

'Anything.'

'Don't let yourself be suckered into anything. Men like Curly earn their pay 'cause there ain't much they won't do for money. Ain't one of 'em you can trust further than the thickness of a dollar bill. I figure you'll be pretty hot on doing something about Curly before long. Fair enough. But don't let him know. Keep it to yourself until you want to make your play. Then go and do it and don't do any hesitating. He won't take much prompting to backshoot you.'

'I'll remember,' Jim said. 'Thanks, Rem.'

'No thanks needed. I'm just protecting my own interests. Remember you're the feller who pays the wages round here.'

Jim grinned. He finished his coffee and prepared to go.

'You heading for Olsen's place?'

'Yes.' Jim shrugged into his slicker. 'Nobody has much faith in the idea. I don't exactly either, but I've got to try and talk with Olsen. I might get him to see sense. Anyhow he'll know that Rocking-T isn't about to sit back and let him take over without a fight.'

14

Once he had negotiated the downward fall of the hills and was on Boxed-O range Jim rode with extreme caution, his awareness of his situation fully realised.

There was no way of anticipating the reactions of any Boxed-O riders he might meet. If possible he intended to avoid any contact at all. To this end he kept close to any cover he saw, riding in amongst any trees or stretches of brush. The dullness of the day and the falling curtain of rain aided his camouflage. Nevertheless he rode uneasily, his eyes searching constantly. Beneath his slicker his handgun was loose in its holster and his saddle-gun was close at hand.

Once, some distance to the north he saw riders plainly outlined against the skyline. Jim pulled his horse close in to a stand of high trees and watched the riders as they moved slowly along the crest of the distant ridge. For a while it appeared as if they might ride his way, but they eventually turned away and went over the ridge out of sight. Jim sat for a while longer, then moved on through the unceasing downpour.

He saw no more riders. In fact he saw no more signs of life throughout the remainder of his long ride to Boxed-O headquarters. Olsen's vast herds were obviously being kept on some other section of the huge, sprawling range.

The complex of corrals, outbuildings, and the huge main house appeared deserted, abandoned almost, to Jim as he crested a rim at the sloping approach to the Boxed-O ranch. He set his horse down the muddy trail which brought him in by way of the maze of corrals and cattle-pens. He passed a large feed-store and stables large enough to hold a herd of horses. A number of wagons were stored beneath a lean-to alongside the stables. It was an impressive setup, Jim admitted. Big, ambitious, built from the dreams of a man who saw everything in a big way.

The rise of smoke from the cook-shack told Jim that someone was at home. He turned his horse that way, dismounting into ankle-deep mud. The cookshack door opened before Jim reached it and a balding, scarlet-faced man with flour-white hands eyed him suspiciously. A cloud of steam billowed out from behind him and the odours of hot food and coffee reached Jim.

The cook eyed Jim for a few seconds. 'I know you, don't I?' he asked.

'You maybe heard of me. Jim Talman's the name.'

The grin on the cook's face was paler than the flour on his hands. 'All I do is make the meals.'

Jim realised that the man was more than a little scared. Trouble of this kind touched everybody involved, from the top right down to the bottom. But he wondered just what sort of a monster he represented to some people.

'Take it easy, friend, I haven't come to shoot holes in your coffee pot.'

A sudden breeze caught the rain and sent it scudding across the puddled yard in a silvery curtain. It struck at Jim, stinging his face and he hunched his shoulders against it.

'Is Olsen at home?' he asked.

The cook shook his bald head. Rain had caught it and it shone wetly. 'You missed him by a couple of hours. Him and the missus. They took the rig and headed for town.'

'Coming back today?'

'Bossman is. I heard he's leaving the missus in town. I figure he wants her out of the way while all this trouble . . . ' The cook's voice faltered and he stared at Jim as though he expected to be leaped upon by a raving maniac.

'I'll try and catch him in town,' Jim said, turning his back on the cold wind that was blowing up.

'You going to stop this mess?' the cook asked.

In his saddle Jim looked down at the man. 'I'm going to try,' he said.

The cook smiled without humour. 'How?'

Jim gathered his reins. 'That's the only part that's giving me trouble.'

'I could get me fired for saying this, but I hope you find a way, Mr Talman, before we all lose more'n we can afford. You know what I mean?'

Jim nodded. 'I know what you mean.' He pulled his horse's head around and urged the animal forward across the yard. Behind him the cook retreated into his warm haven, closing the door against the wind and rain, and the cold, unfriendly world.

Beyond the yard Jim found himself on a regular trail, plainly Boxed-O's road to town. He set himself for another long ride and wished he had taken time to beg a cup of coffee from the bald-headed cook.

Settling himself in the saddle as comfortably as possible, Jim resigned himself to the journey ahead. He was cold and wet, for even the best slicker couldn't keep out every drop of rain; water had somehow got in under his collar and had drawn a chilly finger down his back. The flesh of his face was sore from the constant sting of sweeping rain, his eyes were aching from having to squint and peer through the driving downpour.

He allowed his horse to pick its own way, depending on the animal's instinct to take it on the safest route.

Time dragged as the miles passed by. Jim eased his watch out of the folds of his slicker. He saw that it was after midday, and he realised he must be close to town. Shortly he came onto the main trail and a while later he was passing the first of Garnett's buildings. He was unable to raise any comfort from the fact that he had arrived — each minute that elapsed only brought his confrontation with Olsen that much closer.

He turned his horse in at the livery, riding through the big double-doors.

The large barnlike place was gloomy, deep-shadowed, but it was warm and smelled of leather and horses. Jim dismounted and led his horse into an empty stall. He off-saddled and gave his animal a brisk rub down, then covered it with a handy blanket. He was sweating under the clinging slicker by the time he'd done. Collecting his rifle Jim made for the door, wondering idly where the liveryman was.

At the door he stood for a moment, staring out at the rain-lashed town. He was almost reluctant to go out into the rain again but he knew he had to. Holding his rifle beneath his slicker he stepped out into the downpour and headed for the hotel.

15

Sometime earlier the rig carrying Philip Olsen and his wife had moved slowly along Garnett's main street, coming to a halt before the hotel.

Releasing the waterproof side-hoods, Olsen climbed out and deposited two large handgrips on the boardwalk. He turned back to the rig and gave Victorene a hand down. She walked straight into the hotel, leaving Olsen to follow her, carrying the bags.

Half-angry he dumped her bags by the desk. He was wearing a bright yellow slicker and he was sweat-sticky beneath it.

Behind the desk the clerk straightened his collar and put on a fawning smile as he moved forward. 'Good morning, Mr Olsen. Mrs Olsen. You require a room?'

'My wife does,' Olsen said, his tone

indicating that he was in no mood for trivial niceties.

'Of course.' The clerk made a quick check of his vacancy book. 'Number 38, on the top floor. It has a large bedroom and an adjoining sitting-room.'

'That will do.'

'How long will Mrs Olsen require the room?'

Olsen stiffened, but Victorene smiled gently. 'For some time I think,' she said pleasantly.

'A pleasure to have you with us, Mrs Olsen.' The clerk turned the book for her to sign.

Pen in hand Victorene leaned towards the book. Then her breath caught in her throat, her heart pounded suddenly. She forced calmness on herself and quickly signed her name in the empty space below the book's last entry. An entry which read: Room 35, and was signed Frank Spode. Victorene replaced the pen on the desk and smiled at the clerk. She hoped her feelings were not showing, for despite herself her face felt hot and her heart was hammering wildly. She turned away from the desk and made her way upstairs, Olsen close behind her.

He saw her settled in her room, and it was obvious that he was impatient to leave. Victorene realised quite calmly that her marriage to him was over. She found no sorrow in her heart, for herself or for him. It was as if they were complete strangers, as if they never had been married.

'I'll have the rest of your stuff brought into town first chance I get,' Olsen told her.

Victorene nodded. 'Very well, Philip.' She crossed to the window and watched the rain falling.

'You'll take things from here, then?' he said, and she thought, he even does this like a business deal.

'Yes,' she told him, and her voice had an edge to it that she was unable to conceal. 'Now if you don't mind . . . '

Olsen opened the door, almost eager

to be gone. He glanced at her as if to speak, then changed his mind. He stepped outside and pulled the door shut.

Victorene went to the bed and took off her coat, then returned to the window and watched until Olsen came out of the hotel and climbed into the rig. She watched him turn the rig and drive on up the street to the bank. He got out of the rig and went into the bank.

Once he was out of her sight Victorene put him out of her mind. She went across to the dressing-table and tidied her hair, then left her room and walked down the corridor to the door that carried the number 35. She hesitated for only a moment before she knocked lightly on the door. She was about to knock again when the door opened. 'Hello, Frank,' she said, and, surprised at her own boldness, she stepped into the room.

Frank Spode closed the door. 'How did you . . . ?' he began, but Victorene

170

gave him no more time to talk. She came against him eagerly, her arms going round him and her lips seeking his. Spode pushed his questions aside, gave himself over to the emotions that demanded satisfaction. For a time they held close until their held-back desires could be checked no longer. Words were not needed now, and they gave themselves wholly to each other until they were spent and utterly drained. And then they lay together, bodies close, enclosed in their own world of togetherness. Victorene told him then what had happened, that she was parted from Olsen for good, and for a time it was a hard thing for Spode to realise, but when he did he held her warm, naked body tightly in his arms and made her the promise that he would never leave her alone. Never, he promised, and made the vow that he would kill any man who tried to take her from him.

16

Leaving the bank Philip Olsen drove the rig down to the livery. He had lingered for a talk and a glass of brandy with the bank's manager, but it was still a little way off noon. Knowing Howser and Jarrett though, he thought, they would likely be there in plenty of time.

He drove the rig around to the rear of the livery, parking under the slope-roofed lean-to that was there for the purpose of sheltering rigs and light wagons. He unhitched the horse and led it inside the livery.

The liveryman, an old-timer who seemed to have been in charge of the place for as long as anyone could remember, was raking the hard-packed floor with slow, measured strokes. He glanced up as Olsen led his horse inside.

'Morning, Mr Olsen. One hell of a day, huh?'

'Depends on which way you look at it.'

The old man stopped his raking and leaned on his tool. 'Yeah, I guess so. Course this is what you want, ain't it, water and lots of it, I mean.' He paused to scratch at his thin neck. 'Now me, I could do without it. This kind of weather keeps everybody indoors. Nobody wants to come out in this kind of downpour.' He sighed. 'Just ain't good for business,' he muttered.

'Rain won't last forever.'

The old man nodded. 'Guess you're right.' He leaned his rake against a stall. 'Anyhow, I figure I'll get me some lunch while things are quiet. Just see to your horse first.'

Olsen forced a smile. 'You go ahead. I'll see to it.'

'You sure?'

'I'm sure.'

'Well, if you say so. Thanks, Mr Olsen.' The liveryman shuffled off to his pokey office and dragged on a slicker that practically overwhelmed his skinny frame in its folds. He raised a hand to Olsen as he went out of the door and started up the street.

Olsen put the horse in a stall and gave it a rubdown. As he worked his mind was mulling over numerous problems. At the top of his list was Jim Talman and Rocking-T. He felt a little more satisfied after last night's raid. The running of Rocking-T's herd would keep things on the boil. Olsen had other schemes afoot to pursue his harassment against Jim Talman. With Curly Browning as foreman now, Olsen was anticipating a rapid forward movement of his takeover. Curly was eager to show his paces, willing to execute all the orders he was given. He had led Boxed-O last night, scattering Talman's herd to hell and gone. The shooting of Andy Jacobs hadn't been part of Olsen's plan but he wasn't complaining. It was another prop knocked from under Jim Talman, another weak spot in the structure of Rocking-T. It would be things like those that would win him Rocking-T. Bit by bit, but it had to be done quickly. And if it were not moving quickly enough there was always his final weapon — and the reason he was here today.

The killing of Jim Talman had to be something apart from anything else he was involved in. He would tell no one. The fewer who knew the better, he had decided. His use of Howser and Jarrett would be known to himself and the two men he was hiring. Maybe he wouldn't need them. If he did he would use them without hesitation.

Olsen heard movement behind him. He straightened, turned. Howser and Jarrett stood watching him. A faint smile touched Howser's lips.

'I figured you for a man who paid others to do his work for him,' Howser said, and Olsen sensed the meaning behind his words.

Olsen finished the rubdown. He stepped out of the stall, wiping his damp hands on his kerchief. 'I started out as a stableboy,' he said. 'I know what it means to have dirty hands.'

'Easier to pay to have it done though, huh?' Howser questioned.

Olsen ignored the needling and took a white envelope from his coat. 'Half the agreed sum.' He held back as Howser reached out a hand. 'Understand me clearly,' he told the pair. 'You behave as usual until I give the word. You don't contact me, I'll come to you.'

'Sure. Don't you worry, Mr Olsen.' Howser's eyes were gleaming. 'Hell, we won't foul up.'

'You'd better not. Do this right and maybe I'll be able to use you again.' He handed over the envelope. 'Don't start throwing this around. We don't want anyone starting to wonder where you suddenly got rich.'

Olsen watched with distaste as Howser and Jarrett hungrily divided the money. 'Stay in town and keep handy,' he told them. 'And remember what I've told you.'

'Sure thing, boss,' Howser grinned. He touched the brim of his hat, then turned, with Jarrett following close, and left the stable by the rear door, leaving Olsen alone with his thoughts.

17

Olsen was not at the hotel. According to the clerk Olsen had left after he had seen his wife settled in. Later, the clerk added, he had seen Olsen make his way down to the saloon.

Crossing the muddy street Jim stepped up onto the boardwalk and walked along until he reached the saloon. He paused long enough to remove his slicker. He hung it from one of the hooks provided, then he went inside.

The saloon was fairly busy. Cigarette smoke and the murmur of talk filled the air. It was noticeably warmer than outside. Jim saw a few men he knew and he spoke to a number of them as he passed. They were for the most part ranchers like himself, and they all knew the problem he had. Although none of them actually mentioned it, Jim could tell they were acutely aware of what was happening. Jim could appreciate how they felt. They understood his trouble and they plainly sympathised, but they would not want to get involved. Every man there had problems enough. Getting caught up in another man's range trouble was something none of them needed — or wanted.

Jim would have liked to have stayed to talk with them longer, but he had no time now. He had spotted Philip Olsen. The Boxed-O owner was sitting alone at the far end of the saloon on the raised, railed-off section that was the closest anyone could get to privacy in the saloon. A near-empty bottle stood on the table before him and a glass was in his big fist.

Jim made his way over to where Olsen sat. It had been some time since he had actually seen Olsen in the flesh. From what he saw now Olsen had changed. The man had put on weight, mainly in the face. But Jim didn't let himself be deceived into believing that

Olsen had gone soft. Olsen looked as hard and tough as his reputation had painted him.

Stepping up to Olsen's table Jim pulled out a chair and sat down. For a moment it seemed as though Olsen might ignore him. Then he glanced at Jim, his face taut, somewhat flushed by the whisky he had consumed. A faint smile played across his lips at some silent, inner thought.

'You come to say you've had enough?' he asked.

'I came to see if we can work this out before there's any more trouble,' Jim told him.

Olsen drained his glass. 'I don't see anything to work out.'

'Quit playing, Olsen. Just what is it you want?'

'Nothing more or less than Rocking-T. Lock, stock, and barrel.'

'Just like that?'

Olsen smiled coldly. 'I believe in facts, Talman, hard facts. You got something I want, and I aim to have it.

As simple as that.'

'Not so simple,' Jim said. 'Rocking-T is mine and it stays mine. You expect me to give in just because you make loud noises?'

'It could save you a lot of grief.'

'Won't work, Olsen. If you want Rocking-T, you'll have to get it the hard way. Rocking-T will fight all the way, and play just as dirty as you. That's a promise. I figured it was a waste of time talking to you, but I had to try.'

Olsen sat up straight, his hands flat on the tabletop. 'Look, Talman, why make things worse for yourself. Sell out now, while there's still something left to sell. I'll give you a damn good price, better than you could get anywhere else. Face facts, Talman. I need Rocking-T. My expansion has to be quick, and that means I have no time to play about. You can't fight me. I can beat you in any way. Men or money. You figure it and you'll see I'm right. So why bring trouble on yourself. I'll take you in the end.'

'Big talk,' Jim said, 'but are you man enough to make it come off?'

Anger rose in Olsen. 'That is what you'll find out. You want it the hard way do you? All right, you'll get it. All the way down the line.' He paused for a moment. 'Remember how Andy Jacobs ended up.'

For the first time Jim let his emotions get the better of him. He came up out of his chair with such force that he turned it over. He towered over Olsen, the rifle gripped tight in his hands. He was close to breaking point and he knew it. And it scared him, because he wasn't sure what he might do if he did let his control slip. Olsen must have sensed it too for he turned his face up to Jim, and for a fleeting moment fear showed in his eyes. It vanished just as quickly, and it was the Olsen of old who faced Jim, his broad face tight and totally defiant.

'I won't forget Andy,' Jim said finally, 'or Ben Nolan. By God I won't. You've set the rules in this game, Olsen, so don't cry when you get hurt, because I promise that's one thing you will get.'

Olsen, pouring himself another drink, appeared to ignore Jim's threat. 'You figuring on crying for help to Nolan?'

'You know damn well that Ben Nolan was hurt bad last night. Hurt when he tried to help Andy Jacobs.'

'Things do happen,' Olsen said cooly. 'The cattle business is rough — it's a man's life, but it's rough. Dog eat dog.'

Jim eased off now. He was in control again, able to take Olsen's remarks without flaring up.

'Just keep your riders off my range, mister. From now on any Boxed-O man is fair game for my crew. It'll be shoot first and worry later, and I never meant anything so strong in my life.'

He turned away then, before Olsen could reply. He could feel Olsen's eyes on his back all the way to the door. Outside he retrieved his slicker. It was getting colder, but Jim was glad of the fresh air. He stood for a moment, undecided what to do. Then an impulse caught him and he turned along the boardwalk. His long strides ate up the distance and eventually brought him to John Dobbs' store.

He stepped inside and felt the calm, unhurried atmosphere of the place surround him. He put his slicker and rifle aside and moved deeper into the store, removing his sodden hat. He passed stacked goods and provisions, savouring the mixed aromas, and felt a calmness come over him.

'Anyone at home?' he called.

Sound came to him from the back of the store, then he saw Melanie Dobbs as she emerged from the doorway that led to the living quarters at the rear of the building. A pleased smile touched her lips as she saw him.

'Jim. What a nice surprise. Whatever brings you to town on a day like this?'

He managed a wry smile. 'Haven't you heard what's going on? Or are you just being polite?'

'Oh, Jim, we were so sorry when we

184

heard.' The concern was clear in her tone.

'Thanks for the thought,' he said.

'Come on through,' Melanie said. 'Dad's in the back. I'm sure he'll want to talk to you.'

Jim followed her through the door. A short passage led to the living-room, with bedrooms and kitchen on the other side. John Dobbs was seated before a rolltop desk, busy at work over a thick ledger. He glanced up at Jim's entrance and got up.

'Hello, Jim.' He took Jim's hand for a moment. 'Come and sit down.'

He led Jim over to where a blazing fire roared in the big open hearth. Jim settled himself in one of the two big armchairs and Dobbs took the other.

'Coffee, Jim?' Melanie asked.

'Yes, ma'am,' Jim said, glad that she had asked.

Jim stared at the fire, letting the warmth of it seep into his tired body. Last night and today's long ride were beginning to tell on him.

'How bad is it, Jim?' Dobbs asked, his voice coming to Jim as if it were a long way off.

'Bad enough.' Jim glanced at the storekeeper. 'I don't suppose I need to lay it out for you?'

Dobbs smiled. 'Storekeepers are like parsons. They hear every bit of news from miles around simply because most people come into a store at one time or another, just as they would a church.'

'Then you'll know how things stand right now?'

'The tale is that your neighbour Olsen has made a try at taking over. Tried for your water first, then made a raid on your herd last night.' Dobbs paused, as though reluctant to go further, then added, 'Up to now each of you has lost one man, and the sheriff has been bad hurt.'

'Man just can't keep a thing to himself. Beats me how the word gets out.' Jim leaned in closer to the fire. 'You haven't heard anything on how I can get this settled have you?'

Dobbs smiled dryly.

Melanie returned with a tray holding cups and a pot of hot coffee. Jim took his cup gratefully, tasting the sweet, black brew. It was good and as he drank he began to feel hunger touching his insides.

'What's your next move, Jim?' Dobbs asked.

Draining his cup Jim considered the question. Just what was his next move? It seemed crystal clear. He had to get Rocking-T prepared for a long fight. There seemed no other way. Olsen was all set to keep on raiding anything and everything connected with Rocking-T. Jim had the feeling that from now on things would really hot up.

'Only thing I can do is to keep on fighting. Make Olsen see that if he wants Rocking-T it's going to cost him.'

'Jim,' Melanie asked, 'why has this Olsen suddenly taken it into his head to go for Rocking-T? I mean why now, in such a hurry?'

Jim glanced at her. He became aware

that the question had been at the back of his mind all along. At first it had seemed that Olsen's move had been primarily aimed at Rocking-T's water. The end of the drought had made that excuse void, but Olsen was still pushing, obviously intent on a quick takeover. The question was why?

'I'm still trying to work that out myself,' he said.

John Dobbs was silently drinking his coffee. He put his cup down and produced a pipe which he filled and lit up. He sat for a moment, collecting his thoughts before he spoke.

'I think perhaps I can throw some light on that for you, Jim,' he said.

'I'd be grateful if you could.'

'See what you think of this. While we were on the way here, maybe just over a week back, we passed a trail drive, heading in this direction. And that herd was carrying a Boxed-O brand.'

Jim let the facts sink in. Olsen bringing in a herd. Why? Didn't he already have more beef on his range than the rest of the area put together? Then he began to recall the things he'd heard about Olsen's visit to Chicago. How the man had come back with contracts a mile long. Contracts to supply beef, that would make him a rich man when he honoured them. If he honoured them, Jim realised. Olsen, full of ambition, determined to get on, would do anything to make good on any deals he had fixed. If he required more cattle he was going to need more range, for it was a wellknown fact that he was already overgrazing Boxed-O. Jim brought his suspicions to the point of reality. Now he could see why Olsen needed Rocking-T so desperately.

'What was the size of that herd, John?' he asked.

Dobbs smiled slowly. 'I was saving that one, Jim. I'll tell you something. I've seen some herds in my time, but I've never seen the likes of this one we passed. It was massive. You remember it, Melanie?'

189

The girl nodded. 'I don't think I'll ever forget it.' She turned to Jim. 'It seemed to stretch for miles, and the dust . . . ' She made a distasteful face.

'What kind of beef was it?' Jim asked.

'A mixture,' Dobbs told him. 'Breeding stock and a lot of young stuff.'

'Now it begins to make sense,' Jim said.

'How?' Melanie asked.

'It's known that Olsen has a lot of big contracts to honour with the Chicago meat-companies. In short it means he has to produce a lot of beef within a certain date. That means he has to expand his herds. And that means he's going to need a lot more range than he has at the moment.'

Dobbs was relighting his pipe. 'And Rocking-T is his choice.'

'It figures. Rocking-T is the largest section of range after Boxed-O. Also it adjoins Boxed-O. In fact it's just what he needs.'

'What do you aim to do?'

Jim got up. 'First I'm going to do

some checking up. Try to pin down everything I can about that herd.'

'Then?'

'Then I'll be able to make a move.'

Jim retrieved his hat, saying it was time to make a move for home. He thanked the Dobbs for their hospitality, and also for the word of the approaching herd.

'You go careful now, Jim,' John Dobbs said.

They were at the door, watching the rain as Jim pulled on his slicker, picked up his rifle. 'I will,' he said.

He left the store and began the walk down to the livery. Dobbs' news had given him a lot to think about and he was wholly preoccupied as he strode along. So much so that he was almost unaware at the touch of a hand on his arm. Then it registered and he spun round, suddenly alert, his rifle coming up in his hand.

'Hey, easy, Jim,' the owner of the hand said, and Jim recognised Frank Spode.

'Sorry, Frank. I guess I'm a little touchy.'

'You been talking to Olsen?'

Jim nodded. 'And wasting my time too.'

'He won't budge?'

'Hell, no. He ain't about to let up a fraction. Not until I'm off Rocking-T and he's on.'

'I'd say he was in for a long wait.' Spode pushed his hands deep into his pockets. 'He still in town?'

'Down at the saloon.'

Spode appeared suddenly ill at ease. Jim wondered why, then dismissed the thought. Whatever Spode's problem he wouldn't thank anyone who tried to interfere, no matter what the motive.

'Frank, you know anything about a big herd Olsen might have coming in?'

Spode's troubled look vanished as he nodded. 'I know some,' he said. 'He sent near six to eight men off maybe eight weeks back. Didn't tell me much about it. Olsen's pretty close-mouthed sometimes, even with the people who work with him. I heard some bunk-house talk about a herd being due.'

'Could be important, Frank. John Dobbs, down at the store, told me he'd passed a herd on his way here to town. He didn't know the men, but he said the brand was Boxed-O.'

'Big herd?'

'John Dobbs said so.'

Spode's face sharpened. 'And you figure this is why Olsen's pushing you so hard of a sudden?'

'It figures,' Jim said. 'He'll be wanting extra graze.'

'It fits the pattern,' Spode agreed. 'I guess you've heard about those con-tracts Olsen got in Chicago. They'll mean big money if he comes through. He's ambitious, Jim, and he'll do any damn thing he can to make things work out in his favour.'

Jim nodded. 'That's something I know.' He glanced off down to where the gaudy saloon-front showed through the misty greyness of the falling rain. 'Well, maybe he's about to find out there are folk who're just as stubborn when it comes to the push.'

18

Night was closing in when Jim finally got his horse bedded down in Rocking-T's stable. He picked up his rifle and stepped out into the rain once more, making his weary way across the muddy yard. Lamplight showed in the windows of the bunkhouse and cookshack, pale beams spilling out onto the yard. Ready as he was to get inside the house Jim turned towards the bunkhouse.

About half the crew were inside, gathered round the big iron stove. As Jim stepped inside the aroma of boiling coffee reached him.

'Hell, Jim, you look wetter than a drowned rat,' Saintly Jones drawled.

'Feel like one,' Jim said.

Jan Dorn appeared from the small, closed-off section of the bunkhouse that served as the foreman's sleeping quarters. He was shirtless, his upper body clad in faded, red-flannel underwear. His broad face looked tired.

'Any trouble?' Jim asked.

Dorn shook his head. 'Today is all quiet. We got herd all gathered. Drove them over to east pasture. Couple of the boys will stay to watch them.'

'How many did we lose?'

'No more than twenty head. Is not too bad, eh, Jim?'

'Bad enough.' Jim tipped his hat back. 'No sign of Boxed-O at all?'

Dorn shook his head. 'Nothing. But we don't take chances.' He indicated the men around the fire. 'Soon we ride out. Every man. Ride the boundary lines. We make sure we don't get caught out again.'

'Thanks, Jan.'

'You have good day?'

'Like hell,' Jim told him. 'It's no go, Jan, he won't give up.'

'Ah! Only one way to talk with Olsen. He hit you with rock you hit him with bigger one.'

'I'm inclined to agree.'

Jim told Dorn what he had been told while he'd been in town and what it appeared to amount to.

'This is why he hits us you think?'

'I reckon that's it, Jan.'

'Then he will try again. Soon. Is good we are ready.'

'Maybe we'll be doing some hitting ourselves, Jan,' Jim said. A plan was slowly forming at the back of his mind, brought on by Dorn's reference to the notion of eye for an eye. It was blurred as yet but it was emerging with increasing clarity.

'How so, Jim?'

'Give me time to work on it, then I'll let you know.'

He took his leave then and carried on over to the house. The kitchen door opened at his touch and he stepped inside, feeling the welcome warmth reach out to embrace him. Ruth was there, with her father. They were sat before the kitchen fire, and as Jim came in Ruth's head turned. A soft sound came from her lips as she saw him. In an instant she was on her feet, coming to him and throwing her arms around him, ignoring the wet slicker.

'Hey, take it easy,' Jim said. 'I'm not exactly at my best. You carry on like this and I'm liable to just fall over.' But he was glad to be back with her and his kiss told her so better than any words could.

'I was worried,' Ruth said. She helped him out of his slicker then took him over to the fire and made him sit down. 'Now you stay put,' she told him. 'I'll get your meal ready.'

Jim glanced across at Doc Baily. 'You see what I have to put up with.'

Ruth's father tapped his pipe out against the firegrate. 'You complaining about the way my daughter treats you?'

Jim smiled tiredly. 'Not ever,' he said.

'How'd things go today, Jim?'

'They didn't. Nothing's changed.'

Ruth appeared at Jim's side, a mug of coffee in her hand. 'Wouldn't Olsen listen to you, Jim?'

'No. He's decided he knows what he

wants and he intends to keep after it.'

Ruth said no more as she moved away to prepare his meal, but Jim could sense her unease.

'Doc, how's Ben?'

'He's been pretty restless all day. His wounds are giving him some pain. He's sleeping now. I gave him a draught to ease the pain some. I figure he'll sleep until morning.'

'Would he be able to stand the journey to town?'

Baily nodded. 'If it's taken easy. Why? You want him away from here?'

'You can't stay at Rocking-T for much longer. You've other patients. With Ben in town you'd be able to keep a pretty close watch on him.'

'And?'

Jim smiled. 'And I'd like Ruth to go with you. If things start to get rough out here I don't want her in the middle of it.'

'Are you expecting it to get rougher?'

'I'm not expecting it to get any easier.'

'You think Olsen might bring the fight right to Rocking-T's doorstep?'

'It's possible,' Jim said. 'That's why I want Ruth in town.'

Baily nodded. 'Fair enough, Jim.'

'And what if Ruth doesn't want to go to town?'

Jim glanced round to where Ruth was standing. 'She'll go,' he said, 'because I've said she'll go.'

'Yes, Jim,' she said, and went back to her cooking, saying no more on the subject.

Later, as they lay together in their bed, she held him close to her, and Jim could feel her trembling.

'I can't help it, Jim, but I'm frightened.'

'Easy now. We're doing fine.' He drew an arm around her tightly. 'Leave the worrying to me.'

'Easy to say.'

He kissed her warmly. 'You know, I figure it's time you had other things to occupy your mind.'

Ruth stirred in the dark warmth, her

voice gentle. 'Such as what?'

'Oh, we'll think of something,' he told her. His hand drew the front of her nightdress open, moving gently to the firm swell of her breasts. For a while there was only the whispered sound of their sudden embrace.

'Now you mean . . . ?' Ruth began, then let it trail off.

'Can you think of a better place — or time?' Jim asked, and heard her quick, breathless, 'No.'

19

With Ruth and her father on their way to Garnett with Ben Nolan, Jim was able to concentrate fully on what now lay ahead of him.

The rain had slackened during the night and since dawn it had ceased completely. A pale sun was gradually breaking through, and the morning air had a freshness to it that was welcome.

Buckling on his gunrig as he crossed the yard, Jim watched a pair of riders coming in. He recognised them easily, for Rem Callender's long, lean shape was hard to miss. Jim raised a hand to bring him and Keel over.

'Morning, Jim,' Callender said. He eased himself out of the saddle and took a moment to work the stiffness from his legs.

'The boys take over all right?' Jim asked.

'They did, and was I ever glad to see them.' Callender took off his hat and scrubbed his hand through his hair. 'Hell, but it was wet last night.'

'Rem, I've got a job for you and Josh and me.'

'Sure thing, Jim.'

'You two go and get yourselves sorted out first,' Jim told them. 'Dicken's got breakfast on the go. I'll see you when you're on the outside of bacon and coffee.'

Jim left them and went on across the yard. A number of his crew were saddling horses. Seeking out Jan Dorn he moved over to join him.

'You all set, Jan?'

'Yes,' The Dutchman frowned, scratched his jaw. 'You are sure is going to work?'

'As sure as I can be, Jan. I'll have Rem and Josh with me. Two good men. We'll see it through.'

'I hope so,' Dorn said dourly.

'Look, Jan, we settled this earlier. If we pull this off it'll give Boxed-O something to think about.'

Dorn nodded. 'Yah, you are right, Jim. We do it your way.' He finished tightening his saddle. 'You don't worry. We look after ranch and herd. And we keep Olsen in our sights.'

Dorn unhitched his horse and swung up into the saddle ready to move out.

'Good luck, Jim,' he said.

'And you.' Jim watched as Dorn led the crew out and away from the ranch.

Jim went over to the house and spent some time checking that windows were closed and that the fires were all out. This was something he'd promised Ruth he'd see to. He hoped it wouldn't be too long before he had her back here and they were living in the house like people should, without the worry they had now. When he had finished he made his way over to the cookshack. He found Callender and Keel, changed into fresh clothes, seated at the long table with filled plates of bacon, eggs and potatoes before them. A tall pot of coffee stood on the table between them, and Jim sat down and poured himself a mugful, taking time to taste it before he spoke.

'I've got information that Olsen has a big herd coming in. The way it looks this herd is his reason for wanting Rocking-T. His own range just isn't big enough to carry additional beef.'

Callender continued to eat as Jim spoke. Then he looked up.

'He's a greedy man. What's he after — the whole country?'

'You never can tell. It happens that Olsen was in Chicago sometime back. He made a number of big deals, took on a heap of contracts to supply beef.'

'And that'll mean a whole lot of money for him,' Callender said. 'He's ambitious.'

'I figure what you said before fits better,' Keel said briefly. 'Greedy.'

'Whatever you call him, it still means that to honour those contracts he has to produce a hell of a lot of beef, and that means he needs more grazeland.'

Callender pushed his empty plate

aside and poured some coffee.

'So what do we do?'

'Hell, Rem, I reckon I can figure that out myself,' Keel said.

Jim eyed Callender closely and saw that there was a knowing look on his face. Callender was way ahead of his partner and not too far behind Jim himself.

'We going to throw a little sand in Olsen's coffee?'

Jim nodded. 'That herd is all that Olsen is waiting for, so I reckon we'll do what we can to make that wait a long one.'

'Three of us away makes three less to handle trouble here.'

'I know that, Rem, but it's something I'm prepared to take. Jan and the boys know what we're going to do and they'll hold their end up here. One thing you haven't seen yet is Rocking-T when it's really fighting mad.'

Callender grinned. 'I can imagine it.' He finished his coffee. 'How far out is this herd, Jim?'

'I should say they're due on Boxed-O in three days. That puts them in some mighty rough country just now.' He paused. 'Be a hell of a place for that herd to get to running.'

Keel smiled like a man anticipating an enjoyable task. 'Seems fair,' he said. 'They run off our herd so we give them the same.'

'If we ride steady we should reach it by midday tomorrow. A herd that size will be moving slow. We'll ride as soon as you're ready.'

Keel got up, picking up his rifle.

'We're ready now, Jim,' Rem Callender told him.

20

By the evening they were riding across open, rugged range that lay well beyond even Boxed-O's boundaries. Here the land took on a new face. Gone were the sweeping expanses of grass and trees. This country was heavy with scrub and brush, the beginnings of craggy rock outcroppings. They were heading northwest, and ahead of them the land began a slow climb to the eventual high black peaks of a range of barren, rocky mountains.

They rode for the most part in silence, speaking only when it was necessary. Jim had enough on his mind to keep him occupied, and the two men with him concentrated on their own part in the venture. Keel rode out in front, his keen eyes scanning the country for sign. He was, Jim learned, a born tracker, with a superb sense of direction and the staying power of an Indian. Rem Callender stayed close to Jim, sitting his saddle with a casualness that seemed to verge on downright indifference, but he was as alert as any man could be, constantly dropping back to check the trail behind. Jim realised he couldn't have chosen better men for this particular job if he'd searched for a month.

As darkness approached they halted and unsaddled their horses. Each animal was rubbed down and blanketed, then fed and watered. Only after this was done did Keel build a small fire over which coffee was brewed and bacon fried. A pot of beans went on as well.

Keel ate his meal almost as it cooked, then took a mug of coffee and his rifle as he moved off into the darkness to stand watch.

Ladling beans onto a plate Jim handed it to Callender who helped himself to bacon. Filling his own plate Jim sat back on his heels.

'He always so quiet?'

Callender smiled. 'Josh takes a little getting used to. You know though, Jim, I wouldn't want any other man to partner me. No offence intended.'

'How long you been together?'

'About three years now. First met up down Sonora way. We was both in one of them Mex jails. Both about to get shot too, as I recall.' Callender took more bacon. 'Man, but we were in a mess. They get pretty rough on gringos down there. Anyhow, we figured we didn't exactly favour the notion of being stood to a wall and shot so we made a try at bustin' out.'

'Appears you made it.'

'Hell, yeah. We somehow worked well together. Damn near levelled that jailhouse to the ground. Got us a couple of fistfuls of guns and just shot our way out of there. Found us some horses and burned leather for the border before they knew what'd hit 'em. Since then we've sort of stuck.'

'Sounds a good arrangement.'

Callender exchanged his plate for a mug of coffee. 'I guess it is. It suits our way. We like to move around some, take whatever comes.' He grinned. 'The rougher the better.'

'You'll probably get all the roughness you want when we hit that herd,' Jim said.

'This is going to make Olsen mad as the old maid who thought there was a man under her bed, then found there wasn't.'

'Rem, old maids just won't be in it.'

They rested for two hours then cleared the campsite and rode on. A pale moon came up, painting the land in stark shades of black and silvered greyness. They rode as fast as safety allowed. As the hours passed the air grew chill and they stopped long enough to pull on the thick shortcoats they had tied behind their saddles.

The night passed slowly, without incident, and dawn, streaking the sky about them, found them climbing into stark, sparse-wooded hills.

Once more they halted for a quick meal, washing it down with mugs of hot, black coffee.

With full light on them they rode on, now with increased caution, for they were coming into the terrain where they would find the herd. It had to be in this general area, for this was the only way a herd could traverse these hills.

'From here on in we'd better ride careful,' Jim said. 'We could run into them anywhere around here.'

'I'll find them before they find us,' Keel said. He touched his heels to his horse and rode out ahead of them.

'And he will,' Callender remarked.

'I believe you,' Jim said.

Callender seemed to know which way Keel was going, even though his partner was now out of sight. Jim followed, content to let them get on with a job they plainly knew very well.

He wondered for a moment how things were back at Rocking-T, but he didn't let the thoughts nag him. He had a damn good crew back there, a crew

212

who could handle most anything that came up. Whatever the results of his present action, he knew he was doing the right thing. He was fighting for what was his and as long as he was able he would keep on fighting. This move, if it came off, would hit Olsen hard. It might make him reconsider his intentions towards Rocking-T. Jim knew full well that it might just trigger off more violent action from Olsen, but whichever way it turned out it had to be done.

The morning grew warmer as the sun began to climb. It wasn't long before they were able to remove the coats they had donned against the chill of the night. Though they were on fairly high ground there was no breeze. The air, fresh and sharp, was motionless. Above them the sky was clear, with only a few clouds and it promised to be a hot day.

Hard rock lay beneath the hooves of the horses and the noise of their passage was sharp. Jim began to worry, for sound carried far in this high country. Just ahead of him Rem Callender reined in suddenly. He put up a hand and Jim brought his own mount to a halt.

'You hear something?'

Callender nodded. 'I figure it's only Josh.' He sounded sure, but Jim noticed that he had pulled his rifle from its sheath and had it laid ready across his saddle.

There was only silence. Then Jim detected a faint rustle of sound off to his left. He eased that way and saw Josh Keel emerging from an overgrowth of brush. Keel was on foot, his rifle in his hands, and Jim noticed that he had changed from boots to soft, silent moccasins.

'Set easy, Mr Talman,' he said. He made a swift indicating motion with his hand, back towards the way he had come. 'Back that way. Eight riders and more beef on the hoof than I ever seen before.'

21

'Man, if we get that herd to running they'll be able to see the dust back in Chicago,' Rem Callender said.

Surveying the trailing length of the great herd through a pair of old field-glasses, Jim felt inclined to agree. He had been expecting a large herd, but what he saw now was the largest gathering of beef he'd ever set eyes on. It was only now that he fully realised the scope of Olsen's ambitions.

'I'll say one thing. Those eight riders down there must be damn good to be able to control a herd that size.'

Callender glanced across at Jim. 'Pretty fair,' he said. 'You think we ought to go down and spoil it for them?'

'Hell, yes,' Jim told him and Callender smiled bleakly.

'No doubt as to who they belong to?'

Jim shook his head. 'That's Olsen's band all right. And those riders are all Boxed-O.'

Callender eased back from the rocky rim they were on. Below them the land sloped and dropped away for almost a quarter of a mile to the wide valley floor that cut its way through the range of hills. He studied the lay of the land around them for a minute, then brought his attention back to Jim.

'How do you want to play it?'

'I figure to let them through here. Wait until they get to open ground, then hit them from the rear. Get the herd running, then move out ourselves.'

'That should do it,' Callender said. He looked over to where Keel sat with his hat over his eyes. 'Josh, you game?'

Keel didn't move. 'I'm halfway there,' was all he said.

Pulling a couple of thin stogies out of his pocket Callender tossed one to Jim. They lit up and sat watching the slow moving herd below. Dust swelled up from the hooves of the jostling beasts.

Horsemen rode this way and that, keeping the herd together, making sure that any stragglers were quickly hazed back into the main bunch. Olsen's men were evidently making this drive the hard way, for there was no chuckwagon, and only a small string of spare horses.

It was a half-hour short of noon when Jim decided to move. Before they mounted up each man checked his weapons thoroughly.

'Don't want to sound like a preacher about this,' Jim said, 'but I'm not looking for any human targets down there. The herd is all we're after.'

Callender dropped his handgun back into his holster. 'Kind of depends on how those fellers down there react don't it, Jim?'

'If that's the way they decide to play it, then don't wait. I'd rather no one was hurt, but if somebody has to be then I'd rather it be them than you.'

'Amen to that,' Keel said. He was on his horse now, carrying a cutdown, double-barrelled shotgun in place of a rifle. The weapon looked deadly and very efficient, Jim thought, and realised that the description fitted the man just as well.

They moved out, Jim taking the lead as they negotiated the long slope to the valley floor. The way was unknown to them and they rode with care. A couple of times they found themselves on loose shale drifts and then it was a case of moving with even more caution. Eventually they reached bottom, pausing so that the horses could rest for a few minutes.

By this time the herd was out of sight beyond a curve in the valley's floor. A thin haze of dust misted the air, marking the herd's passage.

Jim gigged his horse into motion, Callender and Keel following close behind. He could feel tension building up inside him now. There was no way of knowing just how this would work out. No one was invulnerable, not even himself. Jim knew this and accepted it, but it didn't lessen the feeling any.

The valley curve was just ahead of them now. They drew rein just before the curve, keeping in the shadow of an overhanging ledge. From where they were they could see the herd without being spotted themselves.

'Couldn't find a better place for it,' Keel said.

'He's right, Jim,' Callender agreed. 'Valley levels out just ahead of the herd. Best way for us is to hit it now, before we come onto that rough country ahead.'

'We won't get another chance like this,' Jim said. He slid his handgun out of his holster. 'Rem, you take the right flank, Josh the left. I'll be the man in the middle.'

'Always had a hankerin' to be in a cavalry charge,' Keel said.

'Don't mind him, Jim,' Callender remarked. 'He just never grew up.'

'Not a bad idea.' Jim drew in his loose reins. 'All right then, let's ride!'

Together they gigged their horses forward, breaking out into the open in a tight bunch before separating. Ahead of them lay five hundred yards of flat, coverless terrain. They had to cover this in the shortest time possible, before they were spotted. Surprise was the mainstay of their attack. If they could reach the herd before Boxed-O saw them, their chances were high.

Jim felt a cold band of sweat streak his back. Now that it was almost on them, he felt a sudden burst of elation, a sudden swelling rise of excitement. He had a fleeting, but clear realisation that this was what Keel had been talking about when he'd made that remark about a cavalry charge. There was obvious danger ahead, pain and possibly even death. Without being melodramatic Jim was able to realise these things, but at the same time he was looking beyond them, to what lay in front and it didn't unduly worry him.

And then there was no more time to think as the tail end of the herd loomed before him. Dust filmed the air around him and Jim dogged back the hammer of his gun and triggered off his first shot. The whipcrack of the gun was loud in Jim's ears and seconds later he heard Callender's first shot off to his right, then the unmistakable twin booms of Keel's shotgun. Jim thumbed his gun's hammer again and fired again, and again. He began to yell. He could hear Callender echoing his shouts.

He suddenly realised that they were pulling it off, for above the gunshots could be heard the frantic bawling of the cattle, a rapidly spreading sound that grew with every second. Steers were easily panicked beasts and fear or alarm in one was swiftly passed to another. Jim knew that it wouldn't take long for the unrest at the rear of the herd to reach the front — and when that happened the whole herd would be off and running.

Jim's handgun clicked on an empty chamber. He jammed it back into his holster and freed his rifle. He one-handed a shell into the breech and loosed the shot into the air.

A dust-lathered steer swung in towards Jim's horse, its eyes rolling and white. It swerved aside at the last moment, plunging off into the rising fog of dust. The incident caused Jim to draw rein and he used the moment to take stock of the situation.

It was plain to see that the herd was on the run. Frightened steers were pushing and prodding at those ahead of them, turning and twisting in their attempts to find some room, anywhere away from the sudden alien noises that had disturbed their calm and placid world.

Jim began to cast about for signs of the herd's attending riders. The Boxed-O men were near at hand and Jim knew that it wouldn't be long before they put in an appearance.

He had less than no time to speculate on the matter for a horse and rider loomed up out of the dust ahead of him. The rider wore a red shirt, paled with sweat and dust — neither Callender nor Keel were wearing that colour. The rider was shouting something but Jim was unable to hear what it was above the din of the stampeding herd. But he could see, and he didn't miss seeing the rider's hand dip and then rise, sunlight glancing off the barrel of a handgun. A flash of flame winked from the muzzle. Jim heard the sharp crack of sound, then felt a tug at his left sleeve. Instinct made him jerk his horse's head round, sending it plunging into the milling herd where the dust was thickest. In seconds he was being carried along by the running herd. His plan to stampede Olsen's beef had worked, but now Jim had other things to occupy his mind. At the moment his main objective was to get clear of the herd and the guns of Olsen's riders.

Gunshots crackled and popped from every direction. Jim wondered how his own two men were faring. He knew Callender and Keel were well able to look after themselves, yet he still worried about them.

Jim began to urge his horse on through the surging mass of steers, hoping to get clear before he was carried too far by the herd's flight. Once the impetus built up the herd would run for miles. Choking swirls of thick dust hampered his vision, clogged his eyes and nose. Digging his heels in Jim gave his horse its head. The animal was used to working cattle and knew instinctively what to do. It sure-footed its way through the herd and almost before he knew it Jim was clear, able to take full control and turn his horse away from the herd.

A shape appeared out of the dust just beyond Jim. He strained his eyes as he tried to peer through the dust. Evidently the other rider was in the same predicament for he pulled his horse over towards Jim.

Jim tensed, gripping his rifle in readiness.

Abruptly the other rider jerked his animal to a halt. In the same instant Jim saw that the rider was from Boxed-O.

Indecision held both men motionless for a second. Then the Boxed-O rider yelled an oath and went for his gun. Reluctant to shoot Jim gigged his horse forward, covering the few yards that separated him and the Boxed-O rider. Olsen's man's hand came up holding his gun just as Jim's horse slammed into his own. The handgun went off with a spiteful crack and Jim felt a hot slash of pain across his left side. Then he was close enough to bring his rifle barrel down across the other's gun-hand. The Boxed-O man gave a pained yell as his gun slipped from nerveless fingers. Jim gave the man no chance to recover. He slammed his rifle across the man's head. No sound came from the Boxed-O rider this time. He simply keeled over and slid from his saddle onto the ground.

Jamming his rifle back into its sheath Jim took his handgun out and made quick work of punching out the empty shells and then reloading.

He realised suddenly that the sound

of the herd had diminished greatly. Jim drew rein on his restless horse, settling it while he turned his attention towards the distant herd. Dust boiled up in great clouds, hiding the herd itself, but marking its passage plainly. Whatever else they had achieved, he thought, the stampeding of Olsen's herd had been absolute. The beeves would run for miles, scattering as they went.

Movement caught Jim's eye. He glanced around. The Boxed-O rider was recovering from his fall. Give him a few more minutes and he'd be on his feet again, and most probably fighting mad. Jim decided it was time to move on.

Gigging his horse forward Jim headed for the protection of the nearby hills. The absence of other Boxed-O riders didn't mean it would stay that way. Any number of them might appear at any moment.

As his horse began to negotiate the lower slope of the closest rise, Jim became aware of a nagging pain in his side. He'd momentarily forgotten about his wound, but now, with the initial numbness wearing off, he was becoming very aware of his injury. He put his hand to his side for a moment and took it away wet with blood. He knew the wound wasn't overly serious, but he knew also that he would be well advised to attend to it as soon as possible.

Only when his horse crested the summit of the farthest level of hills did Jim draw rein. He led his sweating horse into the comparative safety of some close by rocks. He dismounted, laid his handgun on a nearby stone, then got out of his shirt.

As he had expected the wound was not serious. It was only a surface injury. The bullet had gouged a ragged line across his side. It was sore and it was still bleeding. Jim rummaged around in his saddlebags and brought out a roll of bandage, lintcloth and a jar of salve. Uncapping his canteen Jim soaked a piece of the lintcloth and did what he could to clean the wound. He found he was suddenly sweating and a wave of dizziness washed over him. He'd lost more blood than he'd realised.

'Better sit down 'fore you fall over,' a voice said conversationally.

Jim glanced up, his hand snatching for his gun. He had it levelled, the hammer back before his fuzzy mind let him recognise the man who was getting down from his lathered horse.

'Hell, Rem, I wish you wouldn't creep around like that.'

Callender cuffed his stained hat to the back of his head. 'Give me that swab and sit down,' he told Jim. He set to cleaning the gash in Jim's side. By the time he'd finished Jim was feeling a lot more comfortable.

'Thanks, Rem.' Jim eased his shirt back on, standing up to find out if he was less giddy.

Callender, searching inside his saddlebags, glanced over his shoulder. 'I may want you to do the same for me someday.' He came back to where Jim stood, a bottle in his hand. 'Try a bite of this,' he said. 'It'll kick that fog out of your skull.'

Jim took a healthy swallow, then fell to sudden coughing. 'Grief, man, what in hell is it?'

Callender grinned. 'Finest corn whisky a man can buy, Jim. You feel any better?'

'Give me time, Rem, give me time.' Jim handed the bottle back to Callender. His dizziness had almost gone, replaced by a fierce burning sensation originating in the pit of his stomach. 'Where's Josh?'

'He figured he'd trail Olsen's crew for a while. Keep an eye on them.' Callender was sitting on a rock, reloading his rifle. 'Tell you, Jim, that herd is going to run until it hits the gates of hell.'

'Looked that way to me. You have any trouble?'

'No. I guess we just hit 'em so much by surprise those Boxed-O boys ain't yet stopped running round in circles.'

Jim moved over to his horse. 'You ready to ride?'

'Surely. You feel up to it?'

'I'll do.'

They mounted up and Jim led out, following as near as possible the way they had come in. For this part of the ride they were taking to higher ground and after a half hour Jim drew rein. He brought his field-glasses out and had a look at the distant dustcloud that was all he could see of Olsen's herd. From what he could make out the herd was splitting up and going in every possible direction. He handed the glasses over to Callender.

'Olsen is going to be screaming bloody murder,' Callender said softly. 'This is going to hurt him more than anything else you could do to him.'

'That's what I hoped for,' Jim said. 'Maybe this will make him think before he tries anything else against Rocking-T.'

Callender handled the glasses thoughtfully for a time. Then he returned them to Jim.

They rode on, and an hour later they were joined by a grinning, dusty Josh Keel.

'Man, I never seen so funny a sight before.' He took a long drink from his canteen. 'Those Boxed-O riders just don't know what to do. That herd's just running and they can't stop it no matter what they try.'

Jim glanced at Callender and smiled tiredly. He'd done what he'd set out to do. He had hit back at Olsen and he had hit him hard and heavily. Olsen would never forget this, Jim knew, but that didn't worry him. Physical force was all that Philip Olsen understood, so Jim had used just that to hit at him. What would come of this was not yet clear, but whatever it was, Jim decided, he would be ready to fight it. He had put Olsen's back against the wall. Now he would have to be ready to react to the kicks that were bound to come.

Jim gathered his reins and turned his horse towards home. 'Let's go,' he said, gigging his horse into motion, setting out on the ride that would take him to a final showdown.

22

Jim found Rocking-T as he had left it. The ranch was deserted except for the cook, Dicken Hodges, and as Jim, Callender and Josh Keel rode in, he came out of the cookshack brandishing an old double-barrel shotgun. The old man was primed for action and Jim could have sworn that Hodges looked more than a little upset when he saw it wasn't Boxed-O.

'Ease off, Dicken, we're friendly,' Jim said. He slid out of the saddle. 'Rem do me a favour. Saddle me a fresh horse.'

'Sure, Jim. You sure you're all right for any more riding?'

'I'll manage,' Jim said. 'You and Josh get yourselves sorted out and Dicken will get you some food ready.'

Jim followed Hodges into the cook-shack and helped himself to a mug of coffee. It tasted good, better than coffee had tasted for a long time.

'Any trouble, Dicken?' he asked.

Hodges, busy at his stove, shook his head. 'Been pretty quiet. Dutchy and the boys have been in the saddle day and night since you been gone. Olsen's playing it pretty close if you ask me. What do you think he's up to, Jim?'

Jim took another mug of coffee. 'Damned if I know. Maybe he's decided to give me time to think.'

Breaking eggs into a pan Hodges was silent for moment. 'How did your little escapade go?'

'Pretty fair. Olsen's herd got spread every which way by the time we'd done.'

Hodges gave a toothless chuckle. 'Wish I could have seen that. What you figure'll happen now?'

'We'll find out in time. I figure that one of Olsen's riders will make his way back to Boxed-O anytime now. If I know Olsen he'll get every man he can to round up that herd and nursemaid it back to Boxed-O. That should keep him busy for a few more days. Give us a little breathing space.'

Hodges placed a plate of eggs and thick slices of bacon down on the table. 'If you got breathing space,' he said, 'you got time to sit down. If Ruth finds out I ain't been feedin' you proper my life won't be worth a kick in the butt.'

Jim sat down and began to eat the meal with enthusiasm. The ride home had been hard and long, for Jim had set a fast pace. They'd ridden through the night, only stoping once for a quick, cold meal and a short rest. Now the fatigue was catching up on him, but he wanted to get to town as soon as possible. He wanted to see Ruth, let her know that he was all right. He was tired and dirty and unshaven, but those things could wait until he'd seen Ruth.

He finished his meal and left the cookshack, heading for the stable. Rem Callender and Josh Keel came out as Jim started across the yard. He met them in the middle of it and stopped for a moment to exchange a few words.

Later he was unable to remember what was said — within seconds of the conversation starting it was violently interrupted.

Josh Keel, standing a little to one side, put up a warning hand. Callender instantly turned his attention to his partner.

'Riders coming,' Keel said. 'Big bunch. Riding hard. Be over that rise in a minute.'

'Rem?'

Callender nodded. 'If he says so, Jim, they'll be here.'

Jim didn't doubt Callender or Keel. The only question his mind asked was who? And he didn't really need an answer. His own crew would be wide-spread across Rocking-T range, and if they were returning to the ranch there was no reason why they should do so in such a manner. It appeared as if Olsen's laxity had taken a sudden turn.

And then the time for questions was past as a fast-riding group of horsemen burst into view from beyond the rise that Keel had indicated. In the short time left for assessing the odds Jim was able to count at least a dozen riders. They were all well-armed and the way they were handling their weapons it was plain to see that they were out to cause trouble. And trouble was meant to bring grief for Rocking-T.

'Move out,' Jim said. 'Fast.'

The three of them turned, making for the cookshack which was the closest building to them. As they went in through the door the Boxed-O raiders swept into the yard and the first rattle of shots exploded, sending heavy slugs into the plank walls of the cookshack.

Jim slammed the door shut, turned and positioned himself at one of the windows. he heard Callender curse softly.

'Rem?'

Callender, at the window on the opposite side of the door, glanced over at him. 'Just that we got ourselves boxed in tight. No place to make a fight from.'

'Maybe.'

Callender poked his handgun through one of the window-panes, clearing the glass. He loosed off a couple of shots that brought a heavy return fire. 'Jim, we need rifles. Handguns ain't going to do much for us against that bunch.'

Before Jim could reply Dicken Hodges came out of the small store-room. He had a half-dozen rifles cradled in his arms and he laid them down on the table. 'These what you want, feller?' he chuckled. 'Take your pick while I fetch some shells.'

Callender brought two of the rifles over to the front of the cookshack, tossing one to Jim. Keel, who had taken up a position at one of the rear windows, came to the table and helped himself to a couple of the weapons, taking a box of shells from Hodges as the cook returned from his storeroom.

'You can thank Jim's pa for this,' Hodges said. He handed out boxes of shells. 'We've had rifles stashed out ever since way back. Comes from when there were Indians on the loose. We got caught a couple of times, but not after the boss had this notion.'

As he thumbed shells into his rifle Jim turned his attention to what was going on outside.

The bunch of Boxed-O riders, after making their first pass across the yard, had regrouped just beyond the big corral and it was obvious that they were about to make another run. Occasional shots cracked sharply, the slugs smacking suddenly into the walls of the cookshack. One shattered the pane in Jim's window and glass showered into the room.

'What do you figure they're after?' Callender asked. 'Us or the property?'

'I'd say anything marked Rocking-T is fair game,' Jim told him. He levered a round into the breech and watched the Boxed-O riders as they began to round the far end of the corral.

The moment they were clear of the corral, the riders wheeled their horses and set them at a dead run across the open yard. Their way took them past the house first and as they reached it every gun opened up, pouring a hail of lead into the structure. Jim winced as he heard glass shatter. He thought of Ruth's neat rooms, her furnishings and ornaments, and he felt sudden anger rise.

Then the riders came abreast of the cookshack. Their guns opened up again, but this time their fire was answered.

Keel and Hodges had joined forces with Jim and Callender at the front of the cookshack, and as the Boxed-O riders swept by, four rifles opened up on them. Levers were worked as fast as each shell was fired. The noise in the cookshack was deafening and the air became heavy with gunsmoke, the odour of burnt powder.

Keel turned away from the window, smearing blood away from a cut cheek. He began to thumb fresh loads into his rifle. 'Three down,' he said. 'They won't try that again. Next time it'll be on foot.'

Watching the three riderless horses of the downed raiders, Jim felt he agreed with Keel. He switched his gaze to the men themselves. One was dead; he had caught at least three slugs before he'd hit the ground. Of the remaining pair one was kneeling, clutching a bloody, shattered left arm. The other raider lay with both hands held tight against his side. Blood was dribbling through his fingers and the man was cursing loudly, without pause.

Callender listened to the outburst for a minute then called for the man to shut up. The man ignored him. Callender asked again. Now the man began to call his curses at Callender.

'I asked him politely,' Callender said, more to himself than anyone else. He said no more, but simply drew his handgun, aimed fractionally and fired. His shot clipped a slice from the man's left ear. The cursing ceased instantly. The Boxed-O raider threw a white-faced glance towards Callender's window, then awkwardly scrambled to his feet and began an unsteady walk towards his companions who were once more gathered beyond the big corral. The man who remained, realising he was being left alone, also got up and trailed after his injured partner.

'Maybe they'll up and quit now,' Hodges suggested hopefully.

'Don't bet on it,' Jim told him. He was scanning the land out beyond the ranch, wondering if any of his crew were close enough to have heard the shooting. It was possible that they were involved in some kind of trouble themselves. He hoped not. A little while back he had been feeling somewhat more confident, believing that perhaps things were easing off. What was happening now seemed like a direct slap in the face. Jim realised he needed to keep his wits about him if he wanted to come out of this in one piece. Olsen was still intent on his takeover and if Jim let his vigilance weaken it would happen before he realised it. There could be no let up until the matter was settled once for all — one way or the other.

A council-of-war seemed to be taking place beyond the corral. The Boxed-O raiders looked as though they were in disagreement over some matter. Watching them Jim wondered what they were haggling about. He would have given a lot to know.

'Maybe they can't agree on which way to kill us,' Callender said. He raised his rifle and laid it across the window-sill, sighting almost casually. When he fired the sound of the shot was unusually loud in the stillness.

Jim, who had kept his eyes on the Boxed-O raiders, saw one man suddenly jerk sideways and fall from his saddle. The man struck the ground in an ungainly heap, thrashing about wildly until he got his bearings. He sat up, his left hand held around his right upper arm which was blotched with red.

'You figure it wrong to shoot when you ain't being shot at?' Callender asked.

'Is that how I looked?' Jim pulled his gaze from the scattering Boxed-O men. He managed a tight smile. 'I guess maybe I'm not as used to this kind of situation as you, Rem.'

Callender inclined his head. 'I been in a few scrapes, and one thing I learned early was never to wait for the other feller to make up his mind. When it comes to gunplay the one who finishes on his feet is usually the one who shoots first and worries about giving the other feller an even break later.'

And he was probably right, Jim thought, which is why he's still alive.

'Here they come,' Josh Keel yelled.

Callender's accurate longshot had galvanised Boxed-O into action. Now on foot Olsen's men were moving in on the cookshack. Jim saw also an added danger. A number of torches, wood-staves tipped with thick wads of oil-soaked rags, had appeared. It was obvious what they were intended for, and this must have been one of the main reasons for this raid. The firing of Rocking-T headquarters, if it took place would be a shattering blow to all those who worked and fought for it.

'They aim to put us to the torch,' Jim said, anger strong in his words. 'Damn that man to hell.'

'You aim to let 'em, Jim?' Hodges asked.

'What do you think?' Jim said and swung his rifle up. His shot cracked harshly and one of the running men lost control of his limbs, plunging face down in the dirt. The blazing torch he carried cartwheeled for a few yards before it came to rest.

Seconds after Jim's shot the rest of the guns in the cookshack opened up, to be answered by the weapons of the Boxed-O raiders. After that there was time for little else but to aim and fire, reload and fire again.

Caution seemed to have become uppermost in the minds of the raiders. Every man made for the closest cover and then opened up on the cookshack.

Had the cookshack been constructed of lesser material, of weaker wood, the defenders of Rocking-T would have suffered to a greater degree. As it was they came out of it with nothing more serious than superficial wounds. Despite the heavy fire from Boxed-O the sturdy walls of the cookshack kept all but a few of the deadly rifle slugs from getting into the building. Once it was realised that the walls were too thick to penetrate, the raiders' guns ranged in on the windows. Within a short time every shard of glass had been driven from the frames and the frames themselves were splintered and torn.

Jim realised that while he and his men were pinned down, unable to observe what was going on outside, the time was ripe for Boxed-O to move in with their torches. He thought of the house, the barn and stable, the bunkhouse, and all the other structures that made up Rocking-T. Once they were set to burning there would be little that could be done to save them. As he crouched there, hearing the sound of the Boxed-O rifles, feeling the solid smack each time a slug struck home, Jim felt something close to panic begin to build up inside him. For the first time in his life he felt his control slipping. Here was something he was overwhelmingly involved in. His every emotion told him that this thing shouldn't be happening, but downright logic answered that it was. Jim thought about it, forcing himself to calmness. He had to think straight and act fast.

'Rem,' he said, and he knew clearly what he had to do. 'I want you with me on this.'

'On what, Jim?'

'Any time now they're going to start burning the place down. I'm not going to sit here and let that happen.'

'I figured you'd be thinking on those lines.'

'Then you'll know what I aim to do.'

Callender nodded. He finished reloading his rifle, slipped a handful of shells into his pocket.

'Josh, you and Dicken make like we were all still in here,' Jim said. 'Plenty of noise. Give us a chance to get clear.'

For a moment it looked as if Hodges might argue. The old man finally decided against it. 'I'm gettin' too old for them sort of capers,' he muttered sourly.

Jim led the way into the small kitchen, where a window opened out onto the back of the cookshack. The Boxed-O raiders were concentrating their attack on the front of the building and this left the rear open and untouched. It was a bad slip on the part of Boxed-O, but Jim wasn't about to complain. He slipped out through the window, with Callender close behind.

'No messing this time, Rem,' Jim said. 'We'll do it your way. Shoot first, worry later.'

'With fellers like Olsen and the scum he hires there just isn't any other way.'

They moved along the rear of the cookshack, hearing the crackling gunfire of attackers and defenders. Reaching the end of the building they paused. Jim indicated the adjoining building, the bunkhouse, and Callender nodded his understanding. Stepping past Jim he broke from cover and sprinted across the open space. He reached the cover of the bunkhouse without mishap, and Jim watched him move rapidly along its rear. When he reached the far end he vanished from sight and Jim was able to give his full attention to his own part of the job. He could forget about Callender, for the man was more than capable of holding his own in a situation like this.

As Jim turned to size up the lay of the land before him, he saw movement from over by the corral. He saw a man ease up out of the dust and run forward at a crouch, heading in Jim's general direction. Shots from the cookshack kicked up dust close to him but failed to stop him. The man reached the cover of the cookshack and paused there long enough to put a match to the torch he was holding.

Jim had drawn back out of sight and he waited now, his rifle ready as he heard the raider moving his way. The man obviously intended to get around to the rear of the building before he used his torch.

Jim was ready for the confrontation when it happened. The Boxed-O man was not, but he reacted swiftly when he rounded the corner of the cookshack, coming face to face with Jim. The man gave an angry curse and swung the blazing torch up, jabbing it at Jim's face.

Searing heat fanned Jim's face and he instinctively jerked his head to one side, avoiding the direct thrust of the flame. He was not wholly quick enough and the left side of his face suddenly burst into white-hot pain. He lunged forward at the torch-wielder as the man went for his gun.

The muzzle of Jim's rifle was barely in line when he touched the trigger. He felt the rifle jerk in his hands, heard its crash of sound. Through misty eyes he saw the Boxed-O man spin away from him. Jim had shot from extreme close range, no more than a foot away, and the slug took the man just below his ribs on the left side, going right through him, angling slightly so that it came out at the base of the man's spine.

As the Boxed-O man fell, Jim was engulfed by a wave of surging sickness. He leaned his back against the cook-shack wall. The whole left side of his face felt as if it were aflame. His eyes stung violently and his vision was impaired by the fact that everything seemed surrounded by pale, wavering coloured bands. He wanted to stay where he was. He wanted to rest, to ease the pain in his face, but he knew that these things were impossible at the moment. Olsen's men were not going to wait. They were here to cause upset and destruction, and they would if they were not stopped.

Jim knelt briefly beside the man he'd shot. There was nothing to be done, he saw. The man was dead. Straightening up Jim checked his rifle, wondering how many more would be dead before this was over.

A heavy outburst of gunfire sounded from over in Callender's direction. Jim turned that way, crossing the exposed strip of ground to reach the cover of the bunkhouse. A rifle slug tore a jagged chunk of wood out of the log wall. Jim ran the length of the bunkhouse, easing off as he reached the far corner.

A few yards beyond the bunkhouse a flatbed wagon stood on open ground, one end up on wooden trestles. Rem Callender lay in the dust beside the wagon, exchanging shots with the Boxed-O raiders who could be heard by their rifle shots and seen only by the balls of powdersmoke that followed each shot.

Before Jim could intervene the situation altered drastically, a number of things occurring simultaneously.

A Boxed-O man came to his feet and made a sudden dash for the cover of the house. He almost made it. Callender held his fire until the man was within yards of the house, then his rifle cracked sharply and the running man lost his balance and fell heavily.

In the same few seconds Josh Keel, with Dicken Hodges backing him, broke out from the cookshack, their rifle-fire driving the raiders down towards where Jim and Callender had positioned themselves.

And then, coming over the very same ridge that the Boxed-O raiders had used, a small knot of horsemen appeared, pushing their mounts hard as they swept down into Rocking-T's yard.

Jim watched them apprehensively at first, then felt relief sweep over him as he recognised Jan Dorn leading them, with the thin figure of Saintly Jones close by. There were only five Rocking-T riders, but they were enough to tip the scales.

The Boxed-O raiders, seeing the fresh opposition approaching, quickly sized up the situation and decided that things were getting too chancey. As Jan Dorn led Rocking-T into the yard the raiders threw their guns down and stepped into the open, their hands held high.

23

The wounded were seen to first, and then the four dead Boxed-O men were wrapped in blankets and tied across their saddles.

While this was being done the five living and untouched of Olsen's raiders were kept under close watch. Jim finally crossed over to where they were being guarded by Saintly Jones and another of Rocking-T's riders, Henry Teal.

As they crossed the dusty yard, Rem Callender said, 'I see we got Curly Browning in amongst our wild bunch here.'

Jim's head came up. Things had been happening so fast he hadn't paid too much attention to just who was in the raiding party. Now though, his red-rimmed eyes scanned the bunch of dusty, sweat-stained men who stood sullen-faced before him. For a moment he failed to locate Curly, but then he saw him. Jim felt his emotions jar. He was remembering the way Andy Jacobs had died, remembering how he'd found him. Two bullets in the back. Anger rose, swelled up in him. He could almost taste it in his mouth. His right hand moved, his fingers brushing the butt of his handgun. Then he realised what he was contemplating and he steeled himself against the thought. A gun-duel against a man like Curly Browning was nothing less than suicide. Browning was a full-time gunfighter. He lived with a gun, lived by the gun. Jim would be easy meat for him. No, Jim realised, not a shoot-out. Not with Curly. But there were other ways to settle matters. For the first time in his life Jim wanted to deliberately hurt a fellow man, hurt him so he never forgot it.

'Curly Browning, step out here,' Jim called. 'You're safe enough. We don't deal in backshooting at Rocking-T.'

Curly Browning stepped to the front

and faced Jim openly, still cocky enough to sneer at Jim's remark despite his position.

'You accusing me of something, Talman?'

'Damn right I am,' Jim said. 'You killed Andy Jacobs and every man here knows it.'

'Who me?' Curly looked hurt. He turned his gaze on to Callender. 'Hello, Rem. It's been a long time.'

'Not long enough,' Callender said.

'Hell, you still sore about that little mix-up we had over at Kittyhawk?'

'Seems I recall a couple of fellers turned up with slugs in their backs over there as well,' Callender remarked.

Curly's face hardened suddenly. He threw a hard look at Jim. 'The hell with you bastards. One thing you ain't got is proof.'

'I've all the proof I want,' Jim said, 'and that's all I need for the whipping I'm going to give you.'

The coldness in Curly's eyes turned to excited pleasure. 'Why surely,' he said, smiling slowly.

Jim turned to one side while he removed his gunbelt and handed it to Rem Callender.

'Jim, you watch him,' came the soft-spoken warning from Callender. 'He fights to win and he fights dirty.'

'I'll watch him,' Jim said. He took off his hat. To all who were watching he said, 'Stay out of this. No interference.'

He squared round to find Curly. The man was standing motionless, his arms at his sides, big hands bunched into heavy fists. As Jim approached him, Curly suddenly broke into action. He moved fast, his fists coming up seemingly out of nowhere. One caught Jim across the left cheek. The side of Jim's face, already sore from the torch-burn, burst into fresh pain. Tears blinded Jim's eyes and he backed off. Then Curly's second punch caught him a wicked clout on the jaw. Dizziness clouded Jim's senses for a few seconds, and in that time Curly slammed home some hard, swift punches to Jim's body and stomach.

Jim fell back, hoping to gain a little time to allow him to clear his head. But Curly was not giving him any time, he realised. Hard, smashing blows struck him from every angle. Jim felt himself being driven constantly backwards and he knew that if he let Curly carry on this way it would be over fast.

Shaking his throbbing head Jim peered through the veil of tears that clouded his vision. In plain frustration he wiped his hand over his eyes and blinked violently. And suddenly he could see clearly. He wasn't sure for how long, but he knew that he had to make full use of this chance.

Curly, a taut smile on his face, was halfway through a wild, roundhouse punch at Jim's head when Jim halted his retreat. Throwing up his left arm Jim blocked Curly's punch, then threw a hard right to Curly's mouth. Jim felt his knuckles split on contact. Curly gave a strangled grunt as Jim's fist drove his lips back into his teeth. Blood began to flow freely from Curly's torn lips. The blow stopped Curly for one brief second, and it was long enough for Jim to follow up with a slashing left to Curly's broad stomach.

Wind erupted noisily from Curly's bloody lips. He buckled forward, and Jim thought he was going down. He moved in to be close to Curly, but some inner instinct made him pause. At the back of his mind he was remembering Callender's warning. His own caution had come to the fore as well and Jim stepped back and to one side, waiting but ready for any move that Curly might put into action.

Curly had plainly been waiting for Jim to step in close. When he didn't, Curly was left bent over, his hands clasped against his stomach in mock agony. He found himself temporarily high and dry. Sudden rage rose in him and he straightened up abruptly, his broad face more flushed from anger than from pain. His eyes sought Jim, found him and fixed on him. Curly's lips moved in a silent curse and he began to stalk Jim.

Wiping his hands down his pants Jim held his ground, only moving to keep Curly before him. His face burned with pain and the taste of blood was strong in his mouth. A dull ache was spreading across his left side and he knew that his wound had reopened. He wanted no more than to be able to rest, but he knew that there was no chance of that until he had finished with Curly — one way or the other.

Impatience overrode Curly's caution then. He was not a man to whom waiting came easily. In any kind of fight Curly was the type who bulled straight in, using animal-cunning and brute strength. It was a way that brought him a lot of pain, but Curly knew no other and it suited him.

He came at Jim now in a lunge, his big fists swinging wildly. Jim waited until the last moment, then stepped easily to one side, and at the same time he slammed his right fist deep into

260

Curly's stomach. This time there was no faking as Curly went on his knees, gagging violently. Jim turned and got a firm grip on Curly's shirt collar. Yanking the man upright Jim spun Curly round, then released his hold. Unable to stop himself Curly slammed bodily into the rough plank wall of the bunkhouse. Curly clawed at the wall to stop himself falling. Regaining his balance he pushed away from the side of the building and rubbed at the side of his face where the rough boards had scraped his skin raw.

Before Curly had completed his first step away from the wall Jim was on him, his fists sledging hard, punishing blows to Curly's face and body. Curly found himself slammed hard back against the bunkhouse wall, while Jim's fists drove at him relentlessly. When Curly raised his hands to ward off the blows Jim batted them aside without pause. Curly's knees began to sag. In sheer desperation he let himself slide down the wall until his knees touched the ground. Jim's battering ceased momentarily and in that moment Curly threw himself to one side, rolling as he hit the ground.

As Jim turned he realised his mistake too late. Still on the ground Curly drove his booted feet up at Jim's body. In an attempt to avoid the blow, Jim twisted to one side. Even so Curly's boots caught him a stunning blow on the left hip, driving him back against the bunkhouse wall. Off balance Jim stumbled and went to his knees.

Curly was on his own feet by then. Two strides and he was towering over Jim. There was a killing rage in Curly's eyes as he drove his knees into Jim's chest, then followed up with a slamming backhander across Jim's face. Curly reached down and grabbed a handful of Jim's hair. Yanking Jim's head back Curly drove his fist into Jim's mouth.

A burst of pain followed by a spreading numbness engulfed the lower half of Jim's face. He could feel blood coursing freely down his chin from his split lips. He shook his throbbing head, blinking his eyes, and in the second that he opened them again he saw Curly, standing over him, his fist already descending for another blow. Jim threw up his hands in an attempt to ward off the fist. It seemed he would fail, but then one hand got a grip on Curly's wrist. Jim gripped the wrist with both hands, twisting with everything he'd got. A cry burst from Curly's lips as his arm was twisted against the joint. He fought against the pressure for a moment, then let himself go. Jim swung to his feet, following through the movement by letting go with one hand and sledging a smashing blow to the side of Curly's head, sending the man sprawling in the dust.

Curly twisted over on to his back, pawing dust from his eyes. He scrambled to his feet hastily, seeking Jim. To Curly, the fist that struck him seemed to come out of nowhere. It caught him across the jaw and sent him reeling back. He saw Jim coming at him and lashed out wildly. One fist caught Jim a glancing blow on his left cheek, high up, over the bone, and the skin split, blood welling from it instantly.

The pain from the newly-opened gash went unnoticed as Jim continued his advance. Some inner strength drove him on to try and finish this thing. Curly was in full retreat now. He had almost given up trying to ward off Jim's savage blows. His face was streaked with blood, his eyes swollen and puffed. Jim's violent attack was taking its toll of Curly's strength. Repeated blows aimed at his ribs and stomach had rendered him almost helpless.

Staggering now Curly lost his footing and went down on his hands and knees. He stayed where he was, his head hanging, blood dripping from him into the dust. He looked like some old bull tasting defeat for the first time.

Watching him Jim realised that he felt no pity for the man. Surprised at himself, he wondered if all this trouble was souring him, hardening his feelings and emotions. The thought angered him, and he moved forward to where Curly was starting to get up.

Jim waited until Curly was on his feet, then he launched a slamming blow to Curly's stomach. Curly buckled forward at the waist and as his head came down Jim's right fist caught his jaw at the end of a sledging swing. The impact drove Curly upright. He twisted to one side and crashed face down in the dust, one arm bent awkwardly beneath his motionless body.

For a long minute Jim stood where he was. His arms hung at his sides, his head sagged forward. he felt completely exhausted, utterly spent. His body ached from head to foot, every part of him seemed to be hurt one way or another. It wouldn't have taken much to have put him down right then, he realised.

When he moved it was with deliberate caution. Even so he showed nothing of what he felt. Turning to where Rem

Callender stood he retrieved his gunrig and strapped it on with fingers that felt broken in every joint.

To the gathered Boxed-O men he said, 'I want you men off Rocking-T range as fast as your horses can carry you. Tell Olsen what's gone off here today. Tell him this is what will happen every time he tries a trick like this. I'd advise all of you to think again before you take any more of his orders. If he's crazy enough to keep trying that's his worry. But remember it's you men who're carrying the grief home every time. If it was me I'd be figuring whether it was worth the money I was being paid.'

He glanced at Callender. 'Rem, you and the boys see these fellers on their way, will you?'

Callender nodded. 'Pleasure, Jim.' He motioned to a couple of the Boxed-O men. 'You boys can come and pick up Curly. Seems as how he's a slight weary of a sudden.'

Turning away, Jim crossed to the

266

house. He let himself in through the kitchen, making his way to the bedroom. Something broke with a brittle snap under his boot, but Jim barely noticed it, or the other damage done by the Boxed-O rifle fire.

Jim crossed the bedroom, reached the bed, and let himself down onto it. He rolled on to his back and lay listening to the muted sounds that drifted to him from beyond the window. He lay and listened, trying to relax, trying to forget the pain, and without realising it he let himself be taken over by sleep.

24

In the days that followed Boxed-O's abortive raid on Rocking-T, Philip Olsen felt his world starting to crumble around him. Things began to happen that were almost too fast for him.

On the day after the raid, a rider thundered into the Boxed-O yard. Man and horse were both tired and filthy. Olsen came out of the house as the rider almost fell out of his saddle. Olsen had already recognised the man as one of the men he'd sent out on the drive, and he sensed there was something wrong.

'Kirby, what're you doing here? What's happened?'

Red-rimmed eyes focused wearily on Olsen's angry face. 'We got hit,' he said. 'Just beyond Colter's Basin.'

'Hit? Bad?'

'Herd got scattered to hell and back.

Boys are having a rough time tryin' to gather 'em. That country is just one big mess of brush and ravines. I come to get help.'

'You see who hit you?'

Kirby nodded. 'Rocking-T. Jim Talman was there himself.'

A black rage caught Olsen in its grip. For a moment he was at a loss for words. Then he became aware of Kirby's intense gaze. Olsen cleared his mind, ran a big hand through his hair.

'Get the crew together, Kirby, every single man. I want them ready to ride within the hour.'

He turned away before Kirby could say any more. As he made his way back to the house he saw Curly Browning emerge from the barn. Curly's face still bore the marks from the beating Jim Talman had given him. Olsen called Curly over and told him what was happening. Anger coloured Curly's face as he listened.

'Goddam, we ought to burn Rocking-T to the ground and put ropes round the necks of every man who rides for it.'

'Like the last time?' Olsen asked.

The colour in Curly's face darkened visibly. Olsen's words had bit deep. He opened his mouth to speak, then thought better of it. He listened in silence while Olsen gave him his orders.

Returning to the house Olsen made his way to his study and poured a drink. He took it over to his desk and sat down, deep in thought.

First he had to see to the herd. Without it he was practically finished. He had more money in that herd than he liked to think about. Getting it onto Boxed-O range was the most urgent of the matters he had to attend to. After that would come his settlement with Jim Talman. He knew, here and now, that there was only one way to deal with Talman. Once he had the herd safely on Boxed-O he would take a ride into town and have a few words with Dunc Howser and Cal Jarrett. Olsen drained his glass, turned out of the study and started up the stairs.

He left the house some time later and found his crew mounted and ready, his own horse waiting. Climbing into his saddle Olsen nodded to Kirby. 'Lead the way,' he said.

Kirby gigged his fresh horse into motion and the Boxed-O crew thundered out of the yard, leaving only silence and a shifting haze of dust in their wake.

The ride to the herd was long and hard. Olsen maintained a gruelling pace, sparing neither men nor horses, and stops were short and few.

With the onset of darkness the temperature dropped. A short time later it began to rain. Fine mist at first it soon increased until it was a solid, drenching downpour. It was still raining as dawn streaked the sky. The land was overall grey, cold and wet, the earth turned to mud beneath the pounding hooves.

Weariness was deepset in every man by the time the gathering-ground was reached, but Olsen allowed no rest. He took complete control the moment they arrived. No man was spared. Olsen drove them relentlessly. He seemed to be everywhere, giving orders, driving bunches of steers towards the tally-crew. By the end of the day every man on the gather was cursing Olsen to hell and back. Even so they carried on working until darkness and the driving rain forced them to halt. They may have hated his dominance, his orders and exhausting pace, but they were tough, hard men themselves, and one thing they admired was a man of Olsen's breed. Olsen was their kind; he desired something and took it, he wasted no time on niceties. His was the only way to live, the way they themselves lived, and to that end they would stick with him despite the recent setbacks over Rocking-T.

It took the rest of that day and all of the next before Olsen was satisfied that they had brought in every Boxed-O steer that was still on its feet. When the final tally had been made, Olsen found that the stampede had cost him well over a hundred steers dead and nearly forty head that had just plain vanished. Out of the whole herd it was a small number, but Olsen took every lost beef as a personal score to be settled with Jim Talman.

That night he lay listening to the drizzling rain on the canvas lean-to under which he lay. Tomorrow the drive would get under way. Once back on Boxed-O range he would get the herd settled and then he would make the arrangements that would finally rid him of Jim Talman.

Irritation grew in him and he found that sleep was drifting in. What was it about Jim Talman that caused him such discomfort? He stirred restlessly. Most probably it was Talman's stubborn defiance, his total rejection of Olsen's every move against him. The man was a damn nuisance, and as such he had to be removed. When it finally came down to it Jim Talman was just another problem for Olsen, one of many, and like any problem it had to be resolved. Quickly and efficiently. Olsen had realised this and would carry out the preparations as he would for any other problem.

The fact that he was going to have Jim Talman killed in cold blood didn't bother him. But this didn't mean he would let the matter be done openly or carelessly. Despite his power, his ruthlessness, there were still lines he had to be careful about stepping over. His recent visit to Chicago had attained him a lot of influential contacts. He was known by men of power and money, and his way was clear to greater things if he honoured the contracts he had undertaken and proved that he was a dependable man. He was not concerned over news of this range-trouble reaching the ears of Chicago. They knew the way of this hard land and they knew it took a hard man to keep his head above water. Range-wars were part and parcel of the cattle business. If

Olsen came through they would know he was a man who could handle a crisis, and they would not baulk when the time came for more negotiations.

Even so, Olsen realised, there would be no excusing downright murder. If Jim Talman was killed and Olsen was implicated, then he would find that Chicago would disown him quicker than water rolling off a hot skillet. Therefore, the killing would have to be planned and carried out so that he, Olsen, would be left in the clear. He had already made his mind up on how to settle the matter. All it would take to set it up would be a brief visit to town and a short talk with Howser and Jarrett. After that, when it was all over, he could resume his Rocking-T takeover, without Talman putting up resistance.

The sound of a rider coming into camp brought him back to the present. Olsen sat up. He was fully awake and sleep seemed far away. He got up and pulled his slicker on. He crossed to the blazing cook-fire and helped himself to a mug of coffee from the blackened pot that was suspended over the flames. He sat back on his heels and drank the coffee, feeling the cold drizzle wet his bare head.

The rider who had come in appeared on the other side of the fire and took coffee. He recognised Olsen and nodded.

'The herd settled?' Olsen asked.

'Like they were never going to move again.'

The rider drained his coffee, said goodnight, and turned into his blankets.

Olsen stayed where he was. He took more coffee and stared into the flames of the hissing fire. Thoughts drifted through his mind in a slow stream. He wondered about the future, his stake in this growing land. He had a place now and a chance to grow bigger than any man for a hundred miles around. There was no telling what might come in the future. He still had a lot of years in him yet, and many things could happen in those years. He thought briefly of Victorene, and a faint stir of hunger rose in him as he brought to mind the youth and beauty she had, but he knew it was only the want of a man who desired a woman for the physical pleasure she could give him. His feelings for her had never gone deeper. Her strong white body had been the attraction. He regretted losing her, but only because it meant losing the special position he would have had with her grandfather. Olsen shrugged the thought off. There were other bankers who would be eager to welcome him, once he proved his worth. Once he delivered to the Chicago stockyards he wouldn't have to worry. As for the other matter, well, there were plenty of women who would jump at the chance of favouring the bed of a man like Philip Olsen. Money, he knew, could buy a lot of things.

Not Jim Talman though, a needling little voice reminded him. Olsen tensed.

The thought hurt, but it was true. Nothing seemed to influence Talman. Money didn't interest him. Olsen's power, his strength, the size of his operations. None of these seemed to bother Jim Talman. If he was hit he simply hit back. And every man who worked for him seemed to be cast from the same mould.

Olsen emptied his mug. We'll see, he told himself. We'll see who comes out on top. A couple of bullets in the back would soon change Jim Talman's attitude. With Talman out of the way his road would be clear. And then nothing would stop him. Pushing to his feet Olsen returned to his blankets. He dragged off his slicker and lay down. His mind felt clearer now. Tomorrow the drive would get under way. He felt suddenly eager to get started. He wanted to get things rolling. He lay for a while, then drifted into a deep, restful sleep, his confused thoughts sorted out and reshaped into a cohesive pattern.

25

The weather seemed to have settled. The rain looked as if it was going to stop. Overcast skies made the days dark, and the constant drizzle wet everything thoroughly, the ground underfoot becoming sodden and spongy. Grass sprouted thick and green on the hillsides and flatlands.

Sitting his saddle alongside Rem Callender, Jim watched Rocking-T's herd meander about on the plain below them. At least there was plenty of water now, he thought, and ample grass. The rain was becoming a nuisance, but the longer it stayed the better would be the build-up of water.

Jim hunched his shoulders beneath his slicker. He was damp and chilled, his pants below his slicker sodden. 'You fancy coffee, Rem?' he asked.

Callender glanced his way. His lean

face, shadowed by the brim of his hat, broke into a slow smile. 'That is a hell of a tempting offer, Jim.'

'Ain't it just,' Jim said. 'Let's ride then.' He turned his horse towards home.

The past few days had been long and hard. Jim had not been satisfied until his entire herd had been rounded up and moved way over to the far side of Rocking-T range, away from where it bordered Boxed-O. Jim didn't intend to give Boxed-O any more chances at his herd. The final tally showed that Rocking-T's loss had proved to be reasonably light. Jim didn't want another attack on his herd. The next one might not let him off so light. It could happen, and Jim was determined not to be caught out a second time.

Knowing Olsen the way he did, Jim realised that by the time the man had his herd under control and on Boxed-O range, he was going to be close to the end of his patience, and as mad as hell with Jim. One of Jim's riders had seen the Boxed-O crew leaving in a hurry a few days back. Word had almost certainly reached Olsen, and his crew was heading out to gather the herd. Jim hoped that apart from being angry, Olsen might also take some time out to realise that what he had started might not prove to be worth it. It was nothing more than a hope on Jim's part, and he wasn't about to put too much faith in it.

Since Boxed-O's last raid things had near-enough returned to normal. At Rocking-T the everyday routine began to return. Even so Jim made Ruth stay in town. He didn't want her back at Rocking-T yet, not until he was completely certain that there would be no more trouble.

The day after his fight with Curly Browning, Jim had ridden to town. He'd had a strong telling off from Ruth when she'd seen the battered condition of his face and body. Her words had bitten almost as hard as Curly's punches. After Ruth's father had patched him up Jim had gone in to see Ben Nolan. He found that the lawman was making good progress. He was still weak, but he was able to sit up. Jim had stayed a while, then Ruth had called him to eat. She'd got over her anger by then and he sat down and enjoyed a good meal. Despite his protests Ruth had made him stay the night, telling him that the ranch could manage without him for a few hours.

On his way out of town next morning, Jim had seen Frank Spode and Victorene Olsen going into the office of Harvy Lord, Garnett's lawyer. Maybe she was the reason for Spode's reluctance to leave town, he thought idly. He stopped off at the store to pick up a few things and to have a few words with the Dobbs. He'd walked in to find Melanie in the arms of Albert Doubleday, being kissed in a way that explained what was going on better than any words. It made the world seem a little more normal to Jim.

Now as he and Callender rode into

the yard, with darkness falling fast around him, Jim commented on the comparative calm.

'I always feel better when something's actually going on,' Callender said. 'Never did take to waitin'.'

They led their horses into the stable and off-saddled. Rubbing the animals down they fed and watered them, then picked up their rifles and saddlebags and made their way across the puddled yard and went into the bunkhouse. Jim had closed up the house while Ruth was in town. He'd had the bullet-damage put right and then he'd moved in with the crew.

Warmth met them as they stepped inside. Stowing their gear they crossed to the glowing stove and helped themselves to coffee. The night crew were just preparing to move out and were just having a last cup before leaving.

'Take it easy boys,' Jim told them as they shuffled out.

'We'll think about you while we're

out there,' Saintly Jones said. He had a scarf tied across his hat to stop it blowing off and his lean, boney face looked longer than ever.

'Hey, Saintly, get that damn door shut,' someone shouted from the table where a poker game was in progress. 'It's cold in here.'

Saintly uttered something under his breath as he stepped outside, closing the door behind him.

Finishing his coffee Jim went across and watched the poker game for a while, then crossed over to his bunk. He got out of his boots and gunbelt, slid under the blankets and lay listening to the talk and laughter of the card players. He didn't remember who won, for the next time he opened his eyes it was dawn and another day lay before him.

This was the way it went as the next week slid by. A long, busy week as everybody pitched in, the ranch work filling every daylight hour.

Olsen and his crew had brought the

herd onto Boxed-O, and although things appeared to have quietened down Rocking-T kept a watchful eye open.

News filtered in from town as it always had, brought in by Dicken Hodges after a visit for supplies, by a couple of the crew who had decided to ride in one night. For the most part it was just local gossip. Ben Nolan was up out of bed, starting to make a nuisance of himself. A runaway horse had caused considerable damage when it had forced its way into the town barbershop. The tale had it that the barber had been so surprised that he'd cut off the ear of the customer he'd been shaving, but as usual this part of the episode turned out to be nothing more than fanciful embellishment. Albert Doubleday and Melanie Dobbs had announced their engagement. One item caught Jim's attention. It appeared that Victorene Olsen was getting a divorce from her husband. Jim remembered seeing her with Frank Spode, and wondered again how deeply Spode figured in the matter.

Then he received news that interested him deeply, but which also put him on his guard from the moment he heard it.

Breakfast was just over and horses were being saddled up in readiness for the day ahead. Spirits were fairly high, for the rain had ceased during the night and the sun was up already. It looked like it would be a good day, at least as far as the weather was concerned.

A rider came into the yard. He rode over to where Jim stood talking with Jan Dorn. Glancing up Jim saw that the rider was one of Olsen's. The man's gunrig was looped around his saddle-horn. He drew rein in front of Jim.

'I got a message for you,' he said. 'From Olsen.'

'You want to step down?' Jim asked.

The rider shook his head. He'd seen enough of the hostile glances from the Rocking-T crew to know when he wasn't welcome. 'I'll say my piece then go.'

'Say it then.'

'Olsen wants to talk peace. He figures it's time for you and him to quit fighting. Said to tell you he'll be waitin' for you in the saloon come noon, so he can buy you a drink to show he's on the level. And he'll be alone.'

The rider turned away and rode out at a pace that belied the fact that he was trying to appear calm and unhurried.

Jim watched him go. He was trying to put his finger on the crooked card in the hand Olsen had just dealt him, but he couldn't. On the surface the proposition sounded genuine enough. But was it? Jim wanted to believe it. He dare not. It sounded too good to be true. He had to know however. He had to go to town. He could easily be stepping into a trap, but there was only one way to find out. Only one way to answer his questions, and that was to take up Olsen's invitation and make the ride to Garnett.

Despite his crews' disapproval, Jim prepared himself for the ride. He made sure that his handgun and rifle were both fully loaded.

Near enough every man on the crew voiced his objections in no uncertain terms. They were all convinced that this sudden reversal on Olsen's part was a fake, that he was up to something. Jim was inclined to agree, but he knew he had to go. If he didn't Olsen would be able to turn round and say, see, I offered peace, but Talman doesn't want it. Olsen had put Jim right on the spot, and now he was waiting to see which way Jim would jump. Jim wondered what alternative he had, and saw that he was left with a choice of two evils.

Jan Dorn wanted to ride with Jim. It took a great deal of effort on Jim's part to say no. This was something he had to face alone. Dorn saw this in the end, though it was still with a great deal of protesting.

When Jim was mounted, ready to ride, Rem Callender came over to him.

Up to now Callender had stayed well in the background, spending the time attending to his saddle-gun, a fine .44–40 calibre Winchester. Now he wordlessly slid Jim's own rifle out of the sheath and replaced it with his own.

'Bought this rifle a long while back,' he said. 'Got a smooth-as-silk action and a hair trigger, and she shoots straight.' He drew his hand along the smooth-worn stock, then turned away without another word.

This action told Jim that Callender understood the position he was in, and that there was only one thing Jim could do. It was a gesture that he appreciated, coming as it did from a man like Rem Callender.

Drawing his horse's head around, Jim gigged the animal into motion.

The moment he was clear of Rocking-T the build-up of tension hit him. His body tightened until every muscle ached. He became aware of every sound, of every flicker of movement around him. He had released the rawhide loop from the hammer of his holstered Colt almost before he realised he had done it. Sudden self-consciousness washed over him, but he remained openly alert, for he knew very well the kind of target he made out here.

The sun grew stronger. The sky was washed with blue, streaks of cloud marking the paleness. A faint breeze stirred the fresh grass and the leaves of the trees.

Jim let his thoughts dwell on Olsen's offer. What form would it take? It was possible that Olsen had had enough. Perhaps he'd been hit harder than he was prepared for. Maybe he'd figured it was better to quit now, before things got out of hand completely.

Perhaps. Maybe. Jim shook his head slowly. He'd find out the answers soon enough. He felt a sweat-patch forming down the back of his shirt. It was going to turn out far hotter than he had expected.

26

Garnett's saloon was crowded. News of Olsen's offer to Jim Talman had soon got around and whoever was able to spare the time was in the saloon. Whichever way it was called, today would bring a show-down between the two largest brands in the area. This meeting could settle the dispute — on the other hand it might just as well make it worse. Right now it was liable to swing either way. No one knew just how it would end, but everyone was interested. So they waited and while they waited they made use of the time to get in some extra drinking.

On his table at the far end of the saloon, Philip Olsen had a bottle and a glass. The bottle was close to empty. On the surface Olsen appeared calm, even relaxed. In truth though he was keyed up to bursting-point. The whisky he'd downed sat heavily, and he knew he'd been wrong to take it on an empty stomach.

He had a lot riding on what went off today. It was, perhaps, the biggest gamble he'd ever taken. If it came off, all well and good; if it didn't, the hell to it. He'd been a gambler all his life and he'd acquired the mentality that went with it. He figured that he was due to a winning hand about now. Bad cards had been falling his way for too long. This time he had to come out on top. And he could. He'd set this up with too much care and attention for it to go wrong.

A faint smile touched his lips at that thought. The hell it couldn't go wrong. He knew just how wrong it could go. Olsen let his gaze rove across the busy saloon. Bastards. Like a bunch of damn vultures. Everyone of them was going to sit and wait and see how this turned out. He knew they all disliked him, but none of them was big enough to buck him. There was only Jim Talman with enough in him to defy Olsen's Boxed-O. In a way Talman was akin to himself. Talman knew what he had and how to hang on to it. He was his father's son all right. That was why Olsen had to get rid of him. Careful, he warned himself, or you'll bc feeling sorry for him in a minute. He poured himself another drink and downed it quickly.

He'd placed his watch on the table before him, and now he glanced at it. Well over an hour yet until Talman was due to put in an appearance. Only Talman wasn't going to appear. As far as Garnett was concerned Jim Talman would vanish from the face of the earth.

Olsen drew a cigar from his pocket and lit up. He sat back in his chair, wondering just what moment would see Jim Talman's departure from life.

27

'He comin' yet?' Cal Jarrett asked.

From the place they had chosen to carry out the ambush, Olsen's would-be-killers were afforded a clear view across this section of Rocking-T. A few miles farther along ran the regular trail into Garnett. Here plenty of trees and brush gave ample cover, and this was the reason why Howser and Jarrett had chosen it.

They had slipped out of town in the early morning and had found this place without much searching. Concealing their horses in a stand of trees close by they had settled down to wait, taking turns to keep a watch on the approach that would bring any rider their way.

Dunc Howser was close to finishing his watch now and he slid down into the hollow where his partner was stretched out on the ground. 'Ain't a sign of nobody,' he said.

'Maybe he decided not to come,' Jarrett suggested. 'I mean, maybe Talman figures he don't need to parley with Olsen. Hell, Dunc, he's doin' pretty well at Boxed-O of late.'

'True enough. Only Talman's not the kind to drag on a thing like this. If he can settle it peaceful like he will.' Howser took himself a long drink from his canteen. 'Don't worry, Cal, he'll be along.'

Jarrett fell silent for a moment. 'Hey,' he said suddenly, 'what happens if he has a bunch of Rocking-T riders with him?'

A grin creased Howser's unshaven face. 'You look worried.'

'I don't fancy havin' a run in with any of Talman's crew. Hell, look what they done to Olsen.'

'He'll be alone. I know Jim Talman. This is between him and Olsen. Anyhow he won't be too trusting about Olsen's offer. His crew will be watching Rocking-T and the homestead.'

Jarrett still remained a little doubtful. 'Man, I hope so. 'Cause if he ain't alone the deal is off. All the dough in the country ain't no good to a dead man.'

He picked up his rifle and bellied his way up to the crest of the hollow. Scanning the sweep of land before him he watched for any movement. The sun was hot now and he was sweating badly. It ran into his eyes and made them smart.

Time passed slowly. It was very quiet until the distant buzzing of some insect broke the stillness. From time to time a bird whistled, the sound high and shrill.

'Hell, Dunc, I could use a smoke,' Jarrett complained.

'I told you no before. We can't chance anything that might give us away.'

'Christ, Dunc, a cigarette is all I want.'

'Shut-up, Cal.'

'Yeah.'

Jarrett faced about again. He rubbed a hand across his dry mouth, raised his eyes and found himself staring straight at the approaching figure of Jim Talman. For a long minute he lay just where he was, his eyes fixed on the oncoming rider. Then he found his voice and croaked a warning to Howser.

'Where?' Howser asked as he joined his partner.

Jarrett pointed and Howser grunted. 'He's makin' it easy,' he said.

'Maybe too easy,' Jarrett muttered.

'Quit cryin' off, Cal, there ain't no trick. Talman's alone, an' in a while he's goin' to be dead and buried. Now ease over and get ready. When I shoot, you drop that horse of his.'

'Yeah, yeah, I know.'

Jarrett settled himself, his rifle on Jim Talman's horse. And beside him Dunc Howser began to draw a bead on the man himself, waiting for the moment when the range was too close for anything but a hit.

28

Jim had left Rocking-T expecting to get answers, but the way they came almost killed him. At the back of his mind lay the thought that perhaps Olsen had set him up for some kind of ambush. He'd thought about it, but he hadn't wanted to believe it. Even so he had remained on the alert in case something came up. And when it did he was almost caught out.

He got a brief warning, in the form of sunlight dancing on metal. It was only for a second, coming in from amongst trees and brush at the top of a slope some little way ahead and off to his right. As he saw it he thought, damn good place for an ambush, and danger warnings sent his body into action.

Jim kicked his feet free from the stirrups. He grabbed for his rifle and began to clear his saddle. It was then that he felt something slam into his left shoulder. The impact threw him to one side as he left the saddle. As he fell he heard the crack of the shot.

Jim hit the ground hard. His rifle slipped from his grasp. His hat was gone too. He heard his horse shrilling, could feel the vibrations of its hooves through the ground. He forced breath through his body. He realised he had to move quickly. Here he was an open target. He pushed to his feet, snatching up his rifle.

A rifle blasted from up on the crest. The slug struck the earth close to him. Jim turned and ran, making for the cover of a fallen tree that lay to one side of the trail. He threw himself over it, twisting round so he was facing the source of the riflefire. As he raised his head shots tore into the silence. Tree bark and wood chips exploded around him and Jim pulled himself back into cover.

There were two rifles, he realised. The knowledge came as something of a shock to him. He was going to have to play this one carefully. They'd almost nailed him at the first try. Now they would be sizing the situation up, deciding on what course of action to take.

Down on his stomach Jim crawled along to the far end of the tree. Peering around the jagged end Jim eyed the green slope above him. He saw only the tangled greenery at first, with the mass of the background showing almost black. Jim watched, waited, and saw, suddenly, a brief flicker of movement; he saw a man's shirt, the paler blur of the face above it, and again the glint of sunlight on metal. He made no attempt to fire yet. For the moment he was content to watch and to wait for his chance. He had to be sure when the time came. He wanted to see them, for he knew that he would get no second chance.

Pain was filtering through now. His shoulder and upper arm felt sodden. Twisting his head a little Jim was able to see where he'd been hit. He wasn't sure whether the bullet had stayed in, but at least the bone was intact. Fishing his kerchief out of his pants Jim shoved it inside his shirt, pressing it over the wound. He hoped it would help to stem the flow of blood. It would have to do. He had no time for anything else.

He turned his attention back to the spot where the ambushers lay. The man he'd spotted was still there, in the same position. Jim scanned the area around him, wondering where the man's partner was. Was he close by the first man, but out of sight? Or was he somewhere else, moving to a better position?

Jim's question was answered by the sharp crack of a rifle from a position some way off to the left of where he lay. The slug struck the tree above Jim's head and he jerked back instantly, but not before he'd spotted where the shot had come from.

They were on the move. And that meant he was going to have to be ready.

Jim levered a round into the rifle's breech. His left arm hurt him badly, but sheer determination made him lift the rifle.

Another shot crashed out, sending more wood-chips into the air. They were trying to flush him out, make him show himself.

Maybe he ought to, Jim thought. He couldn't stay here forever. He glanced up at the sky. the day was getting warmer all the time. He could end up shot or he could end up dead from the heat.

He crawled back to the end of the tree, eyes searching. The first man was still in the same position, head and shoulders an indistinct shape amongst the foliage. Jim eased his rifle into position, aimed briefly and fired.

The crash of his shot was echoed by one from the rifle of the second man. Jim felt it tug his shirtsleeve. He arched around and fired at the source of the shot. He fired again, then moved back to his original position as he heard a hoarse yell of anger, coming from the place where the first ambusher was concealed.

A figure burst out of the brush on the crest, rifle in hand. Blood made a bright smear across one cheek. A growth of whiskers darkened the man's face, but Jim easily recognised Cal Jarrett, and thought that at least this told him who the other man was.

Jarrett began firing as he stumbled downslope. He was yelling too, in a half-angry, half-confused way. His shots were wild, but still too close.

Coming to his feet Jim swung his rifle on Jarrett. He knew he was presenting himself as an open target to Howser. It was a risk he had to take.

'Hold it, Jarrett,' he yelled. 'Quit or I'll drop you.'

He might just as well have told the sun to stop shining. Jarrett, his face glistening with sweat, came on. He was at the bottom of the slope now, no more than twenty-feet from Jim.

'Goin' to get you, bastard,' he

screamed. 'Bastard . . . ' He lunged forward, working the rifle's lever.

Jim knew he had only seconds to make his choice. It was him or Jarrett.

Jarrett's rifle tilted up a little. His eyes were bright, too bright.

The rifle in Jim's hands crashed out its shot. He levered and fired again before the first ejected casing hit the ground. His first shot caught Jarrett in the left side, just above the hip. The next one hit him lower, smashing his thigh-bone. Jim was close enough to see the slugs punch dusty holes in Jarrett's clothing before the man fell.

Jim was still levering his rifle as he spun away from Jarrett. His searching eyes found Dunc Howser as the man stepped out of the undergrowth. Howser held a rifle in his hands and he threw it aside as he saw Jim.

'You're a hard man to kill, Talman, but I aim to do it. You man enough to face me?'

'I don't have anything to prove,' Jim said.

'Me neither, only I don't aim to let you take me in.'

Jim watched as Howser moved down onto level ground. 'One thing.'

'Ask it.'

'You doing this for Olsen?'

Howser smiled, 'He pays well.'

'I figured that was it.'

'He set you up good. Right now he's sitting in town playing peacemaker, knowing right well you ain't goin' to show.'

'Then I'll just have to disappoint him,' Jim said.

Howser smiled again, shook his head. 'Can't oblige,' he said. 'See, I got a date with him. Got money comin' in on your hide an' I don't aim to miss out on spending it.'

He went for his gun as he spoke, and he was fast, but not fast enough.

Jim shot him where he stood, triggering his rifle from hip level, his shot taking Howser in the chest, knocking him to his knees. Howser still tried for his gun, getting it halfway clear before Jim put another shot into him. This time Howser toppled over onto his back. His body arched violently, then collapsed in the dust, and by the time Jim reached him Howser was dead.

29

Philip Olsen's watch read twelve twenty-five. Eying it Olsen felt a surge of elation race through him. Jim Talman should have been here by now. Obviously Howser and Jarrett had carried out their part of the bargain. Olsen cautioned himself against being too sure. Something could have gone wrong. The plan could have misfired. Olsen glanced across the saloon. The place had quietened down. Everyone was waiting now. He looked at his watch again. He'd give it until one o'clock before he made his exit. By then something would be settled one way or the other.

Through the open door of the saloon he could see out onto the dusty street. All he needed to see was Howser and Jarrett ride by. Just a simple thing. He felt in his pocket for another cigar.

Biting off the end he reached for a match. The sound of it striking and bursting into flame sounded abnormally loud. Olsen realised that the saloon had gone utterly silent. He raised his head — and held it in surprised shock; the match dropped from nerveless fingers.

Supporting himself against the doorframe was Cal Jarrett. He looked a mess. His face and clothing were dust grimed, and his left side, from the waist down was a mass of blood.

Olsen found himself turning his gaze from Jarrett to the man who now appeared by Jarrett's side. Dusty and with a blood-stained shoulder, hatless and dishevelled as he was, Olsen had no difficulty in recognizing Jim Talman. A coldness swept over Olsen. There was a look in Jim Talman's eyes that told Olsen more than words could ever express. It was a killing look, and it told Olsen that this was one thing he wasn't going to be able to talk his way out of.

The cards had fallen and he'd been

dealt a losing hand again. Anger swept aside his other feelings — anger at himself, at Jim Talman, at everything and everybody. Yet, even while his anger rose he was figuring what he might salvage from all this. Talman was still alive — but so was he, and while he still lived there was always another day. He hadn't given up yet. By God no, not by a long way.

He focused his attention on the two men by the door. Talman had moved forward, pushing the stumbling Jarrett before him. His voice broke through the silence.

'Jarrett, here, has something he wants to say.'

Swaying unsteadily, his hands clasped to his bleeding side, Jarrett muttered a few words. He turned to look at Jim. 'You hear,' he said loudly. 'I need a doctor. I'm bleedin' to death.'

'Say your piece,' Jim told him. 'Say it before I finish what I started out there.'

'All right, all right,' Jarrett yelled. 'Goddam you, Talman.' He turned back so that he was facing Olsen across the saloon. 'He done it,' he said, pointing a bloody hand at Olsen. 'He set up this whole deal. Fixed it so it looked like he was ready to talk peace, then paid me and Dunc to kill Talman and bury him where nobody'd ever find him.'

All eyes were suddenly on Philip Olsen, and he felt the open hostility in them. The way things were going his future was being reduced by every heartbeat. Right now all he had to concern himself with was the way out of this. If he managed to come out alive, then he could worry about his future.

Olsen got slowly to his feet. His eyes were searching the saloon for a way out. The door was effectively barred by Jim Talman. There were stairs to Olsen's right, but he discounted these. Getting himself trapped up there was a sure way to finish himself off. As he rose to his full height, his searching mind recalled the window at his back. Beyond was the alley, running the length of the street.

Once out there he could make for the livery, get his horse. If he could reach Boxed-O he would be in the clear. His crew would back him, and with them at his command he could dictate terms. It would be an easy thing to recruit more men of the type he needed. With them behind him he might yet achieve his desires.

Jim Talman, perhaps suspecting some sudden move by Olsen, eased forward, putting up a warning hand. 'Hold it, Olsen. You don't walk away from this one.'

But Olsen was committed now. His course of action was decided, and he acted without pause. His right hand swept his coat aside, snaking his gun free of its holster. The hammer was back well before the weapon was levelled. Olsen snapped off two swift shots, not waiting to see if he hit anyone. He spun on his heel and hurled himself bodily through the window.

As Olsen crashed through the window, Jim, his own gun in his hand, turned and ran out of the saloon. He had a fleeting glimpse of Cal Jarrett spinning around, his face a bloody mask from being hit by one of Olsen's bullets.

Jim hit the boardwalk and went onto the street. He paused for a moment, indecision holding him. Which way would Olsen go? The answer came swiftly, spurring him into motion. The livery. Olsen would want his horse.

He ran, his boots slapping the dust up in fine clouds. Each step caused a fresh jolt of pain to explode in his shoulder, but he kept running, ignoring the hurt. He knew only one thing — that he wanted Olsen, wanted this man who had coldly ordered his death. He wanted him and he wasn't about to let anything get in his way.

Midway down the street Jim stopped. Somewhere along here Olsen would have to leave the protection of the buildings to cross over to the livery. The question was where? When?

Jim moved slowly on, his eyes

searching each shadowed alley between the buildings. He noticed how deserted the street was, then remembered that it was always this way each day between noon and one o'clock; Garnett had always clung to the midday siesta and for once Jim was thankful for this tradition.

Movement caught his eye. Jim glanced up. A single horseman was riding down the street, coming Jim's way. Jim watched his approach, for the newcomer was a familiar rider.

The rider drew rein some distance from Jim. He sat his saddle easy, eying Jim coldly. He wore a gun on his hip and his right hand was close to the butt. It was Curly Browning. Curiosity shadowed his face as he took in Jim's appearance and his behaviour.

Olsen suddenly appeared, coming out of a narrow alley. He was level with Curly, some way ahead of Jim. He saw both Jim and Curly the instant he emerged from the alley.

'Hold it, Olsen,' Jim yelled. He hoped

Olsen would heed his words, but even as he spoke Olsen was moving.

Dirt streaked his face and marked his clothing. He'd lost his coat and hat. The left side of his face was scratched and bloody. He looked a different man — not scared, but becoming more desperate as the minutes passed. He'd got into something deep and now he was trying to get out, still believing he could come out on top.

'Olsen!' Jim called again.

This time Olsen did stop, but only to turn towards Curly. 'Take him, Curly, take him!' he yelled.

As if Olsen's command had all he'd been waiting for, Curly let out a savage cry. He drove his spurs in and let his horse run free at Jim. At the same time he went for his gun, bringing it to bear and firing. His aim was upset by the moving horse. He fired twice more, his anger mounting rapidly.

Curly's third shot was his last. Before he could pull back the hammer for a fourth, Jim, who had stood fast through the attack, levelled his own gun, took steady aim and loosed one shot. The slug took Curly directly over the heart, the force of it knocking him out of the saddle. Curly hit the ground on the back of his neck and he was dead before his body stopped rolling.

Before Curly's riderless horse passed, Jim was moving up the street, thumbing fresh loads into his gun. He could see Olsen, now on the boardwalk, some distance ahead. Olsen had seen Curly Browning's demise and he was doing his best to keep away from Jim.

Jim could see the livery now. If Olsen got in there it would be one hell of a job flushing him out. The livery-stable was a huge place and there were a hundred places for a man to hide. With this thought in mind he increased his pace.

Olsen turned without warning, his gun exploding with sound. The slug was close. Jim dropped into a crouch, lifted his gun and returned fire. He saw Olsen stiffen momentarily, then watched as the man supported himself against the boardwalk's porch railing. Still unsure of Olsen's condition, Jim rose slowly, his gun ready in his hand. He moved onto the boardwalk, advancing cautiously.

When Jim was no more than ten feet away, Olsen lifted his head. Pain was strong in his eyes and on his broad face. He was grey and sweat ran freely from him. A thin trickle of blood showed at the corner of his mouth. He stared hard at Jim as if he didn't recognize him, then gazed out beyond the town, to the wide, empty land beyond. Only now did Jim see the great wet patch of blood on his shirt, just above the waist.

'I could have been big,' Olsen said then, his voice steady, still bearing the arrogant tone, though even this was quieter now. 'You hear me, Talman? I could have been goddam big.'

'You're big enough,' Jim said. 'why not be satisfied with what you've got.'

'Satisfied? Hell, man, the ones who are satisfied are ten to the dollar. They're the little ones who grub around and just manage to survive. They never do anything worth remembering, never leave anything worth seeing.'

'And what will you leave?' Jim asked. 'I'll tell you. You'll leave a lot of grief and misery, but I don't think many will weep over your grave.'

Olsen's head came round, his eyes blazing with renewed hate and fury. 'Then I won't go alone, by God,' he roared, and Jim saw the gun he still held as Olsen's hand shoved it forward, his finger pulling on the trigger. The gun went off and Jim felt a burning pain explode just under his heart. He felt himself fall, hit the boardwalk. Above him he could see Olsen aiming his gun again. Everything seemed distorted, out of proportion. The muzzle of Olsen's gun looked enormous, the barrel incredibly long. For a moment Jim felt helpless, then he remembered his own gun. He brought it to bear, thinking all the time that he was too late, that Olsen would fire first. And then his gun went off and kept going off until it clicked on empty chambers.

Jim remembered little after that. His last clear image was seeing Olsen falling away, his face a ruined, bloody mask, bright blood pumping out of his chest. And then the whole world spun into fiery darkness and Jim, drained of everything, let go and slid into that darkness.

Epilogue

Summer slid away and before long the days held a touch of winter. The nights grew longer and frost began to show each morning. The ranches around Garnett began to prepare for winter. In mid-November the first snow fell. By December the weather had settled into the pattern it would follow for the next long months.

Despite the fact that snow lay thick on the ground, Garnett's lawman, Ben Nolan, made the trip out to Rocking-T for Christmas Day. He was well over his injuries, but he walked with a slight limp that would be with him for life.

In Garnett the Christmas festivities were well under way as Nolan left for Rocking-T.

John Dobbs celebrated with his daughter and his new son-in-law, Albert Doubleday. The pair had been married two months before, and one of the things John Dobbs had given the couple was a new sign for the front of the store. It read: Doubleday and Dobbs.

In the Garnett hotel dining-room Frank Spode had more than just Christmas to celebrate. Victorene Olsen had returned from Chicago a few days back, her affairs concerning her marriage to Philip Olsen now settled. Boxed-O, now renamed the Bar-S, would be titled over to Spode when he and Victorene were married in the spring. Olsen's death had been the end of Boxed-O's threats. The crew of roughriders had been sent packing and a regular crew had been hired. The huge herds had been cut down to a size fit for the range available and the Chicago contracts had been renegotiated.

It began to snow just before Ben Nolan reached Rocking-T, but the welcome he received on his arrival did more than just make up for the discomfort of his long ride from town.

The big main room of the house, decorated and warmed by a huge log-fire was packed. The entire Rocking-T crew were there, every man looking as if he'd just stepped out of a barbershop. The entire crew was clean-shaven and had combed and trimmed hair. They were, to a man, enjoying themselves like there was no tomorrow.

Ruth was there too, passing round drinks, laughing and looking more lovely than Nolan had ever seen her. He wasn't sure whether it was despite the fact that she was five months pregnant or because she was five months pregnant. Whichever way it was, he decided, it was a good thing to see. Ruth showed her pleasure too when she saw him, coming over to kiss him and make him welcome.

'You sure you're not overdoing it?' Nolan asked her. He knew he had developed a mother-hen attitude towards her. He knew it, Ruth knew it, and so did everybody else, but Nolan didn't give a damn.

'Ben, I've never felt better,' she said. 'Now you give me your coat and go warm yourself by the fire.'

'I brought you a present,' he said. 'If it doesn't suit you can change it, Melanie said.'

She took the gaily wrapped parcel, her eyes sparkling. 'Why, Ben, I wouldn't think of changing it. Thank you. I'll give you yours later.'

'I've got something for Jim too,' Nolan told her.

Ruth smiled. 'He's over by the fire.'

'How is he?'

'Much better,' Ruth said. 'You know Jim. He's as stubborn as you. He just won't quit.'

'He's a Talman, Ruth.'

Her head came up, eyes bright and proud. 'I know, Ben,' she said, 'and I wouldn't have it any other way.'

He nodded. He moved across the room, greeting and being greeted by the men of Rocking-T, and it took him some time to reach the big stone fireplace.

Jim was there, filling a worn pipe from a pouch of tobacco. He glanced up at Nolan's approach and his face showed his pleasure, his smile warm. Even so, Nolan could still see the thinness in his face, a thinness that was only just beginning to fill out. It had been a long haul for Jim, up out of the pain and weakness that had been the aftermath of Olsen's last bullet. No organs had been damaged, no permanent injury caused, but he had lost a lot of blood, and at first it had been thought he'd lost far too much to be able to recover. But Jim Talman was too much of a fighter to let go. He'd fought, for he had a lot to fight for. A home and a wife, a future. And when Ruth told him about the baby he had another reason for hanging on. He was almost back to normal now, though a day in the saddle still left him weary. He tired quickly, but he was gaining strength from day to day.

'Hello, Jim.'

'Ben.' Jim put his tobacco pouch

aside. 'Glad you could make it. Wouldn't be Christmas without you.'

'I figure it's one to remember.'

Jim nodded. 'Amen to that. Though I wish Andy were here to say it for me.'

'He'd be proud to know you came through.'

'I'm pretty glad myself.'

'Hey, I near forgot.' Nolan handed over the parcel he held. He watched Jim open it, saw his knowing smile.

'Brandy, eh. I reckon I'll have to give you an invite to come over and help me drink it.'

'Why the hell do you think I brought it?'

Jim placed the bottle on a table under one of the windows. The falling snow caught his attention and he stood watching it for a while. Nolan, beside him, let the silence drag on for a time.

'What does it tell you, Jim?' he asked.

'Same as always, Ben. It doesn't make much difference what we do, that land out there just goes its own sweet way. Rain, shine or drought. What happened this year hasn't really changed a thing.' He glanced at Nolan, smiling for a moment. 'Tell you what, Ben, I wouldn't have it any other way.'

Nolan nodded. 'Me neither. Mind, I won't forget this year in a hurry.'

'Hell, no,' Jim agreed. He turned then, seeing Ruth coming towards them, a filled glass in each hand. 'Tell you something else, Ben,' he said. 'I don't think I'm going to forget the next one either.'

We do hope that you have enjoyed reading this large print book.

Did you know that all of our titles are available for purchase?

We publish a wide range of high quality large print books including:
Romances, Mysteries, Classics
General Fiction
Non Fiction and Westerns

Special interest titles available in large print are:
The Little Oxford Dictionary
Music Book, Song Book
Hymn Book, Service Book

Also available from us courtesy of Oxford University Press:
Young Readers' Dictionary
(large print edition)
Young Readers' Thesaurus
(large print edition)

For further information or a free brochure, please contact us at:
Ulverscroft Large Print Books Ltd.,
The Green, Bradgate Road, Anstey,
Leicester, LE7 7FU, England.
Tel: (00 44) **0116 236 4325**
Fax: (00 44) **0116 234 0205**

Other titles in the
Linford Western Library:

BAD DAY AT
AGUA CALIENTE

Daniel Rockfern

The Department of Justice wanted Yancey Blantine badly! The killer and his renegade crew had wiped out a town and slaughtered everyone in it, before running for the shelter of Mexico. The Attorney-General gave the order to follow Blantine's trail and bring him in alive. He knew one man who could do it — Frank Angel — but he also knew what trouble Angel would face. Meanwhile, through the wild and empty land, the Blantines put out the word . . . kill Angel!

TRAVIS

Richard Wyler

Jim Travis had every penny of his hard-earned savings in Sweetwater's bank. It was his future — but when Luke Parsons and his wild bunch cleaned out the town's bank, Jim's money was part of the haul. With no help from the town, Jim rode out to retrieve his money, trailing the Parsons bunch across wild territory. Parsons threw everything he had at the lone rider dogging his heels, yet Jim kept on coming — and forced a final, savage showdown.